ZE
DAWN.

-1-

Aloy sat on the cliff side of Mother's Watch, her knees huddled to her chest as she watched the morning sunrise take flight over the horizon. The sky spilled into a multitude of colors as the warmth of the sun fell gently across her face and the cool mist of freshly fallen snow was carried up in a soft wind that soothed her skin from the heat.

All Mother's temple lay shrouded below her for she had climbed higher than normal simply wanting to escape the confines for a few hours and the pesterings of her tribe that so desperately sought her forgiveness for...well, everything; Lansra more than anyone. She didn't want this. She didn't want to be this "Anointed" character that was met with bows and praise and cries of exultation everywhere she went. She hated it, all of it.

These same people shunned her ever since she was born, refusing to even acknowledge her existence let alone make eye contact with her. And god forbid one of them actually speak to her. Rost was her only family. He was all she needed. And now he was gone too. She found hypocrisy to be extremely inundating but through her travels she met plenty of people who suffered from it. But this, all of this, was too much. And it made her angry.

It had been nearly a week since the destruction of Hades. She felt...lost, now. Ever since Rost was killed she had a goal of avenging his death, finding Helis, which turned into something far larger and more important than she ever dreamed possible: saving the world. Again. But it was a goal, wrapped into several mini-goals along her path to finding the secrets of Gaia to discovering the knowledge of Elisabet Sobek to learning the downfall of the old ones thanks to Ted Faro and his corporation to finding her own roots of creation. Everywhere she went, there was always something new she found, something new to accomplish or figure out or someone new to help. Now? Now there was just...nothing.

As a seeker she trekked across the entire state seeing lands and machines that did more than just take her breath away. She stopped the destruction of the planet, she destroyed Hades, she saved Meridian, she managed to keep all of her friends alive in the process. She then returned to Mother's Rise and was forever revered as The Anointed often seeking council with the Matriachs who deferred to her for everything. And now here she was, sitting way out of reach of all of them.

There was still one thing that constantly ate away at her mind, one she found silly but altogether refused to ignore. Elisabet Sobek. She saw the holo-vid, how she walked out into the scorching, machine infested Earth and sacrificed her life so the entire world could live. But a part of Aloy's nagging mind refused to believe that she actually died that day. She was too smart for that. And Aloy wanted to find her. Sylens be damned, she believed Elisabet was still alive and she was the closest thing to a mother Aloy had. She had herself a new goal.

She closed her eyes and sighed laying on her back as she watched the morning clouds roll by. A scrambling to her left caused her ears to prick on alert but didn't turn to see who it was that was climbing up to her and interrupting her brief moment of solitude. The figure slumped clumsily down beside her and laid back on his elbows.

"Hiding in plain sight so they won't find you?"

Aloy looked over to see Varl smirking down at her.

"Oh, you know me. Hide in the last place people will think to look. Plus if I climb high enough the matriarchs can't reach me."

He let out a small chuckle.

"They look up to you, you know" he said gently

"They were throwing things at me and ready to shun me a month ago."

"They fear what they don't understand which...is pretty much anything new. But you're turning that around. You're shedding off these old ways and traditions that really needed to change and people are actually listening to you and agreeing with you. You could make some serious headway if you keep it up."

"And what do you think of all this?"

"Personally? I think it's refreshing. Change isn't always bad."

"At least you stopped bowing at me."

"That's why you're so perfect for this, Aloy. You don't want all this power when you have no idea how much you really have. You're humble and that's something this tribe desperately needs."

"No pressure" she huffed.

"Look on the bright side, at least Lansra is terrified of you now. She bows every time you walk past her, afraid you're gonna smite her."

"Yeah...I'd by lying if I didn't find that a little satisfying" she replied, a guilty grin playing across her face.

"Have to say though, I'm surprised you didn't climb higher. Don't get me wrong, getting up here was a pain in the ass but you're Aloy the swift and nimble who can calm machines with her mind and shoot an arrow in half. This is sub par for you."

"Oh, is that what they're saying about me now?"

"They also claim you can sing a Thunderjaw to sleep and surf a Snapmaw's back down a waterfall."

Aloy rolled her eyes.

"Wait, are you telling me those things about you aren't true? Think of the children, Aloy."

She smacked him playfully on the shoulder and he pretended to look hurt.

They sat in silence for a few minutes simply staring out over the horizon before Aloy looked up and quietly said: "I just like the view from here."

Varl looked over at her realizing her face had become crestfallen. She was hard to read sometimes but Varl liked to think he almost had her figured out. Almost.

"You really miss him, don't you?" he asked softly.

"Everyday. I think about what he'd say if he could see me now. If he'd be proud or...betrayed. I don't know."

"Why do you think he'd feel betrayed?"

"Because I'm practically a sovereign of the very tribe that outcast him for trying to avenge his family."

"I didn't know him but he did a great job of raising you. You saved the world, Aloy. Not many parents can boast that of their kid. My mom would give me a slap on the back and say 'praise be to All Mother for assisting you' and that'd be it. He'd be more than proud, I know it."

"Except he wasn't my dad, not really. He raised me, taught me everything I know but if you look at blood-"

"Blood doesn't make someone you're family."

"I was made from a machine, Varl" she said, looking at him with saddened eyes.

He inched closer and let his arm drape over her shoulder.

"That doesn't make you any less human" he said gently, "It just makes you...you."

"I don't feel human. I didn't have a mother who raised me like you did or even any semblance of one. I was planted in some metal embryo and dropped out like a robot. I just wish there was someone I could be traced to, someone I could physically see and feel."

"What about Elisabet Sobek?"

"She died."

"But you don't believe that."

She looked at him surprised, like he could read her thoughts. He really was getting better at this.

Varl was her closest friend. He knew everything; Elisabet, Aloy's origins, how humanity was almost destroyed the first time. He even knew about Gaia. Aloy created her in a sense. She was made to finish was Elisabet had started and she was the only who could. Telling the rest of her tribe this would destroy them, however. There was nothing above All Mother and no one created All Mother. All Mother was just...All Mother. There was no questioning it. And as angry as she was at them for some things she could never just shatter their belief system like that. All Mother gave them hope, gave them a reason for living and fighting and for doing practically anything and everything. Aloy couldn't take that from them.

Varl had come to her a few days after the battle. He had had some doubts. He simply asked if there actually was an All Mother. Aloy had told him there was if he wanted there to be. But that didn't satisfy him so she told him the truth. He was taken aback at first and then just looked...sad, disappointed. But he believed her. All Mother wasn't as complex as he originally was brought up to believe but she still gave life to everything on the planet, including himself in a way and that made him feel somewhat better.

It was refreshing for someone else to know all this information. Aloy was eternally grateful for his friendship.

"I have hunch" Aloy relented.

"Tell me" he said excitedly.

"You know she walked out from Elysium and all the alphas in the room believed she had died?"

He nodded for her to continue.

"I don't think she did. I think she found a way to survive. Maybe she had another bunker or she never actually went outside and only wanted them to think she did. I think she's still alive. She found a way to stop an endless hoard of machines from destroying the planet, she could have easily found a way to preserve her life too. She was a genius, that would be child's play."

"But where do you think she would have gone?"

"I'm not sure."

"What was that thing you told me about once? How the old ones could freeze themselves and stay alive but...not?"

"Cryogenics?"

She had only heard the term once, she was surprised she still remembered it.

"Yeah. Maybe she did that. Uhh...how do you do that?"

"I'm guessing she was put into some sort of metal embryo like I was born in and...frozen somehow without being able to melt. She would have to be sealed in pretty tight. The question is, where do you go for something like that?"

"She was pretty close to All Mo-...Gaia" he corrected himself, "Maybe it was somewhere near her. Maybe Gaia was the one who monitored everything and made sure she was okay."

"But I've been there. I've been in her office, I've talked to Gaia. She wasn't there."

"She had to have gone somewhere no one would think to find her. So where's the last place you hide where no one will think to find you?"

Aloy paused and then looked him incredulously, "In plain sight."

"What say we go take a second look at that mountain?"

"It's a pretty hard climb" she mused.

"Pfft, don't insult me, Aloy" he grinned, "The real challenge is gonna be getting out of here without being seen."

"I thought Sona put you on guard duty for the week?"

"Oh, she'll most definitely try to murder me if and when she catches me buuuut...this is a little more important in my opinion. Uh, that is if you actually want company. I know you're used to doing these things on your own" he said, nervously placing a hand on the back of his neck.

"No, I want you to come. Maybe you'll see something I missed the first time. Plus singing to Thunderjaws is really tiring when I'm the only one doing it. Strains my voice, you know."

He laughed and answered casually, "well then lets go, can't keep them waiting."

They managed to make it halfway down the outcropping before diving into a flood of bushes as they waited for the matriarchs to enter the sacred mountain.

"Do I look alright? Am-am I wearing too many beads, is that allowed? Will the Anointed forgive me for bumping into her this morning...Oh All Mother I hope I didn't bruise her! she shrieked.

"Hush, Lansra" Teersa jeered, "You're giving me a headache" the old woman groaned, rubbing her temples as her sister matriarch fell to her knees for the twentieth time that day to ask All Mother to ask The Anointed to please have mercy on her.

Teersa dragged her up and into the mountain much to the old woman's protests who kept pleading to the heavens to not smite her for entering.

From the bushes Varl covered his mouth to stifle a laugh while Aloy pinched her nose in annoyance and shook her head.

He touched her arm and pointed out of the foliage indicating that their path, for the moment, was clear. They crouched behind a pair of tents, Varl leaning carefully around one side and then motioning for her to follow. He looked to the guard tower and noticed his mother standing resolutely at watch like a statue, a very deadly statue that he was sure was probably getting more than annoyed at his absence. He was supposed to have checked in ten minutes ago. Sona had upgraded. She still carried a bow but she decided that a sword made from the entrails of a Deathbringer was was not only a suitable war trophy but also a suitable weapon that made her look twice as fierce and ten times as intimidating. She kept it slung across her back for the most part but now she was twirling it in her hand.

Varl gulped and kept moving.

"You don't have to do this. I don't want to get you in trouble" Aloy whispered, following his gaze.

"This is way more fun" he smiled, "besides, she can't do too much. I'm accompanying The Anointed after all."

"Good point. If she murders you, I'll have to smite her. She scares me so I'll have to do it in her sleep."

"You, the all powerful Aloy afraid of the little ol' war-chief?" he grinned.

"She does this thing with her eyes. If looks could kill I'd be dead ten times over now."

"I know that look. That look froze me while I was taking a piss once and then it froze my piss."

"Do I-?

"Nope, probably not. I missed guard duty check in by a minute that's all you need to know."

Aloy shook her head in bewilderment before continuing forward. She could see the entrance gate in plain sight, it was only twenty steps away at most. It probably would have been easier to just tell her tribe that she was going on a journey for a few days and wasn't sure when she'd be back and was taking Varl along because she needed his help but a part of her still wasn't used to that form of regalia and she much preferred to be in her own element which was not only the hard way but the sneaky way. Varl didn't complain, he was the same way. They were hunters after all, sneaking was practically in their blood.

Rather than heading straight through the exit the two of them clambered over the side of the wall in the far corner of the village where no one could see and once they were both over and in the clear they shot off like whizzing arrows and headed toward Gaia Prime not even once looking back.

-2-

As it was custom for the Nora to always carry their weapons, even at home, Aloy and Varl thankfully didn't need to stop and grab them before darting out of their village.

The trek would be long and cold. But mostly, it would be high. They stopped several times off the main path to set up camp and warm themselves by a fire as they waited for night to engulf them.

In the distance the sound of Striders could be heard clunking through the grass among their loyal watchers who kept vigilant as they ate. The machines themselves seemed much less hostile since the downfall of Hades. It wouldn't be right to call them outright friendly, exactly, but approaching them didn't always result in an attack anymore. The Watchers would merely look at them and then continue their duties of monitoring. Their eyes would flash yellow from surprise but quickly return to their relaxed shade of blue. The larger machines however, Aloy still wasn't sure about.

Just to be on the safe side however, they set up camp far away from them just in case they decided to turn volatile in the middle of the night. Varl slung his bow and skin of arrows gingerly to the ground and slumped in front of the fire warming his hands.

"So what happens when we actually find her? What do we do?"

Aloy joined in beside him outstretching her hands. She appreciated the fact that he used the term when rather than if.

"We have to be careful and considerate. She'll be really confused and probably scared."

"Right" he nodded in agreement, "Gotta say, I'm a little nervous, ha. What's she like? The woman who essentially created All Mother?"

"She's really no different than you or me. She's human, she's just incredibly smart. And she loves helping people, she loves caring for people and doing what's right even if it goes against the odds."

"She doesn't sound all that different from you" he poked her in the shoulder playfully.

She cast her eyes to the fire and smiled, "I don't even know what to begin to say to her...or ask her" she said quietly.

"Starting with a name is always a good place."

"So much has changed since her time, people have

changed."

"Then we take it step by step and we fill her in a little at a time. Where are we gonna take her? The Nora isn't fond of new things, remember?" he simpered.

"I don't think taking her to a tribe is really the best idea anyway. I was thinking about going to Meridian. Avad would be more welcoming and if I tell him she's important to me, he'll look after her."

"Don't tell my mom this but...I kind of like Meridian" he smiled guiltily.

"But Meridian is full of weakness, Varl. What would Sona say?" she gaped.

"Sona would say I better pray to All Mother for strength before I get used to all that comfort" he chuckled, "But...I guess I can't really do that anymore" he finished quietly.

"I'm sorry, I never should have told you. I didn't want to take that away from you."

"No, no" he corrected her quickly, "I'm glad you did. I don't want to live in a lie or pretend to worship something that isn't even there. That's not strength, that's just dependance."

"Still though, you went your entire life on that belief system and I ruined it for you."

"It's not like you tied me up against my will and made me listen, Aloy. I asked you for the truth."

"And I shouldn't have told you."

"But you're a good friend so you did."

"There still is an All Mother, Varl. She's not a spontaneous being who came out of nowhere but she still exists. She still renewed the planet, gave life to it, provided us with everything to survive. I've seen her, I've heard her speak and she's...kind and nurturing and wants the best for everyone here, wants them to be happy and healthy and safe. She's not so far off from what the Nora taught you and there's nothing wrong with wanting to pay homage to her."

He nodded deep in thought as he processed all that she said. Aside from Aloy, he was the only one who knew the truth, not even the Matriarchs were aware just how high on the scale of nature Aloy actually was.

"You never told me how you felt about All Mother" he began, "Did Rost ever tell you about her or make you believe in her like the tribe did?"

"I...believed in myself. Rost had a firm belief that she played a part in everything, even things that I did completely on my own with no help whatsoever. But I was a little more doubtful, I didn't really think she existed and if she did...I didn't think she guided my every move. All the training I went through, all the lessons I learned, all the progress I made, that was all me. I didn't have any help, I just...did it."

"We never really had a choice. Sona taught my sister and I all about ever before we were even walking. It just became routine after that."

"You took the truth surprisingly well" she said gently, "I know it must have been really hard to hear."

He sighed, "It makes sense. But instead of thanking All Mother for everything, I guess I should really be thanking Elisabet Sobek. If not for her, none of us would be here."

"You'll get the chance" she smiled, "just don't bow" she finished with a wince.

"Ha, no promises" he grinned.

Before too long the fire crackled away and they both fell asleep. They woke to the sound of a fox mewing and birds chirping and realizing it was morning, gathered their things and continued their journey.

The sun continued to shine and light their way and Aloy was thankful it hadn't snowed or rained on them so far. The Sacred Lands were renowed for its unpredictable weather and there was nothing Aloy hated more than being drenched from melted snow. It put an entirely new definition to the term "cold".

She remembered the way to Gaia Prime as if it she had made the journey yesterday. They passed beyond the borders of the Sacred Land and Varl hesitated before stepping his foot over. Aloy had outlawed the rule that Nora tribesmen would be outcast for venturing beyond their territory and it was one that Varl still wasn't quite used to.

A few days later they journeyed to Meridian, stopping along the way to observe how much more peaceful the various machines seemed to be. Where Sawtooths once pounced at the chance for attack, they merely glanced at them before continuing on their way. Where Glinthawks would have dove head first to the ground without hesitation at the sight of humans, they no longer gave them the time of day. Of all the machines Aloy was forced to battle on her path to saving the world, the Glinthawk was by far her least favorite. Mostly because they attacked in groups and were too cowardly to fight on the ground, so Aloy would be forced to tie them down which usually resulted in being swept off her feet by the second or third that was accompanying her victim after they dove headlong into her abdomen. It was a very annoying and painful process.

After passing through the Meridian gates and being greeted by the guard's pounding of halberds, they strolled to the marketplace and split off. Varl went to stock up on supplies and inquire about a new bow and Aloy strode to the palace steps and sought council with King Avad. Upon seeing her presence the guards bowed respecfully and immediately let her pass.

Itamen, Avad's younger brother whom Aloy and Vanasha had smuggled from the Shadow Carja kingdom of Sunfall was busily playing in the garden's below Avad's throne, the older man looking down at him with a smile as he chased a ball happily along the shallow river border. His mother looked on with a smile too, finally seeming at peace and safe.

Hearing footsteps, Avad turned and upon seeing Aloy pulled her into an embrace.

"My friend!" he smiled, "How are you? Sit, sit" he motioned as he strode to one of his couches. It was still healing but Meridian had come a long way in just a few days. Most of the wreckage had been disposed of and not surprisingly, by the Oseram. They never wasted scrap, managing to salvage pretty much anything they could get their hands on. It wouldn't suprise Aloy if Petra came calling with an entirely new species of weapon after all this. She was good at that.

Avad looked happy. There was plenty of room in his palace for Itamen and his mother and Avad was just glad to have the company. He was a lot different from his father, something the two of them desperately needed and were extremely grateful for.

"I'm doing well Avad, how are things with you and Meridian going?" Aloy asked.

"The cleanup process is a mess, everyone is working round the clock. But we're getting there, slowly but surely."

"Have you had any more trouble from the Shadow Carja?" she asked, nodding her head in the direction of his new house guests.

"No, thankfully. With Helis gone most of that rabble has died down. They're just now letting their guard down, nothing is going to take them from here, not if I have any say in it. Thank you for bringing them here, I never got a chance to tell you that with everything going on. I'm grateful, as are they."

"It was no problem. I'm glad I could help."

"So" he said after a pause, "The Anointed, now? How does that feel?"

Aloy rolled her eyes, "Like a massive headache that never goes away. Is that what it's like to be a king?"

He laughed, "I think it's worse. To be revered as a king

or revered as a god..." he balanced his hands ,"think I'll go with king."

"It's definitely something I don't think I'll ever get used to, that's for sure."

"It can be a massive pain in the ass at times, but it can also bring a lot of good. I changed a lot of my father's cruel ways because I had the power to. I don't regret that for a second. But, I doubt you're here to listen to me ramble on about being king. What can I do for you, Aloy?" he asked with that same smile he had when they first met.

"I have a request" she said quietly.

"You need only ask" he answered without hesitation, "After everything you've done for us, for this city, whatever you need, it's yours."

"I'm trying to find someone and when I do, I just want to be sure they're taken care of. I can't take them back to the Nora, it wouldn't go over well right now. So I was hoping they could stay here under your protection where I know they'd be safe and comfortable."

He looked ecstatic, "I'd be honored. Any friend of yours is a friend of mine and rest knowing they'll be well looked after. I built a guest wing in the back there" he said pointing towards his palace, "It was meant for you when you passed through if you ever wanted to stay and I'd be more than willing to house them there" he smiled, "It's the least I could do."

She sighed with relief, "Thank you, Avad. That means a lot to me."

"If you don't mind me asking" he began hesitatingly, "I mean, if there's anything I can do to help please let me know."

"I have an idea where she is, I just hope I'm right. But she is important to me and I need to know she'll be safe."

"There's nowhere safer, you have my word."

She nodded, satisfied.

"I only wish I could go with you" he groaned, "I'm due for a little adventure."

Aloy raised an eyebrow in suspicion, "Are kings allowed to have adventures?"

"Only ones that aren't dangerous, which means they aren't worth having."

"What if I brought an adventure to you?"

"Through your friend? She must be quite the character."

"She's more than that. But you'll have to see for yourself when I find her."

"Well what are you waiting for then?" he smirked, "Bring me an adventure" he nodded toward the entrance way.

Aloy chuckled and bowed sarcastically on her way managing to get another laugh from him in the process. That's what she liked most about Avad, he was a king but he was modest. He had humility that kept him down to earth. He took things seriously when he had to but he also knew how to be playful. He was also generous, selfless and incredibly kind, which is why Aloy knew Elisabet would fit in perfectly here.

She caught up with Varl at the marketplace. He managed to find himself a new bow, which he really needed after the fight with Hades. His old one was close to snapping in half and at this point it was beyond help of fixing.

"Goodbye Violetta" he sighed, easing his old bow gingerly into his pack as he slung the new one over his shoulder.

"You named your bow?"

"You haven't?" he gasped.

"What is it with men and naming their bows?" she asked incredulous, thinking of Nil.

"A bow is like a good woman, Aloy. You gotta treat her with respect and give her all the adoration she deserves and then it's only right that she has a name. She's not an object after all" he said as if Aloy should have already found this to be obvious.

"Right" she murmured, "What was I thinking?"

She motioned to the one across his shoulder, "So what're you gonna name that one?"

He looked at her taken aback, "You can't just name a bow you just bought. You have to develop a relationship first, learn her kinks and the way she moves when you fight, get to know her a little."

Aloy blinked at him unsure of how to respond, so she merely asked, "Shall we continue then?"

He nodded and followed suit as they both exited the marketplace and after a few paces, Meridian itself.

Three days later they found themselves with a face full of snow as they climbed ever higher up the cliffs to Gaia Prime. The last time Aloy had make this trek she was uninvitingly greeted by a Stormbird, she was hoping beyond anything that wouldn't happen a second time. She had this thing with birds: she hated them. A Stormbird was the equivalent of a flying Thunderjaw and she wasn't in the mood to fight one right now.

Varl was keeping pace with her, this was probably the highest and most treacherous climb he'd made and it was in the book for one of the most difficult for Aloy too. It was easy to slip which Varl nearly did a few times but always managed to find his grip on a ledge below and hoist himself back up.

Their fingers and hands were on fire from the cold, the snow biting into their flesh like a million tiny knives pricking at their skin. Varl grunted as he landed roughly against the cliff face having jumped from the opposite side as he grabbed tenderly to the rocky outcropping to keep himself steady.

"Almost there" Aloy called down above the roar of the wind storm.

"Already?" he replied, "I was just starting to have fun."

"Just a few more feet" she affirmed. She could see the opening in sight and so far all was silent, no sounds of Stormbirds or any machines really. The first time she came here, the place was infested. It may as well have been nest. Now it was a ghost town. There was nothing, not even wildlife to be found.

After a few more leaps and bounds Aloy and Varl clambered to the top and looked out over the horizon. Varl took a breath in wonderment.

"Wow" he said quietly, "I see why you climb everywhere now. You really can't beat those views."

"Wait until you see what's inside."

He looked into the entrance nervously, unsure.

Noticing this, Aloy said sympathetically, "You don't have to do this. It's a lot to take in. It's a lot to process."

He shook his head, "No, I've come with you this far, I'm not gonna leave you hanging now. I need to finish this."

"Are you sure?" she asked again, "I'd understand."

"I'm sure" he confirmed, "lead the way."

Aloy nodded and motioned for him to follow. Gaia Prime was large, it was practically a maze but she could still remember the same path she took almost a week ago to find its core. They passed through the familiar rooms the alphas were housed in. Aloy kept walking having seen it all before but Varl was turning in complete circles trying to look at as much as possible as he took it all in. This was as close to anyting the old ones had created he had been in contact with and he had the same look of curiosity and amazement that Aloy possessed when she entered her first ruin. They were alike in many ways, the least of which was their thirst for knowledge.

Aloy stopped outside the final door, it had seemingly closed again since her time there, the familiar red reticule once more appear over the front waiting to be unlocked. She turned once more to face Varl.

"This is it. This is where Gaia is. Are you sure-"

"I'm sure, Aloy" he answered sternly but sincerely. He knew she was only trying to look out for his best interests.

She took out her spear and pushed one end into the door waiting for the reticule to wrap itself around and unlock. A few seconds later, it turned green and door slide open to let them pass. Aloy entered first, walking to Gaia's core as if she had been here a dozen times before. Varl slowly stepped through the door trying to remember how to breath, let alone how to walk. He was wracked with nerves and trying really hard not to show it.

Finally he came to stand beside Aloy as she knelt down to inspect the core. She furrowed her brows, checking every inch to see if there was something she missed the first time, but there was nothing out of the ordinary.

"Maybe we are just wasting our time. It's been hundreds of years, maybe she did die."

"It can't just be that simple" Varl assured her, "There has to be something we're missing. You read her journals, what did they say?"

"It was mostly about her childhood. Before she went outside she told the alphas she wanted to go home. I went to her home, there was nothing there. It's like you said, if she was frozen, someone had to have kept an eye on her all these years and Gaia was the only one capable of doing that because she outlived everyone. I think I was meant to wake her up, I'm the only one able to get in here. She had to go where no one could find her, none of the other alphas would have been able to enter the core, they didn't have the authority or the credentials. Maybe she knew what Ted was planning, but if she did, I don't understand why she wouldn't save the others from suffocating."

"Maybe it's a lot more complicated than we think. If she's anywhere, she's gotta be here."

Varl took a step back to help her search catching his foot on a stalagmite and tumbled to the groud with a dull thud, his face coming in contact with the underbelly of the core. He shook his head to knock the stars away being careful not to touch anything and furrowed his brows in confusion as he looked at the underside of what was supposed to be Gaia, well, at least what was supposed to have housed Gaia. In the very center he noticed a reticule, red, like the one on the outside of the door and his eyes widened with surprise when he realized that what he was seeing was also a door.

Aloy turned upon hearing him trip and before she could ask if he was alright, he propped himself to a standing position and said:

"Aloy, you might wanna look at this"

She knelt down and saw what he was referring to her. She tried to push her spear to it but it was too long to it under the gap. She realized Elisabet had a fail safe. If someone had managed to breach the door, they would be stopped from going further and finding her. Of the many palm activated holograms Aloy had employed throughout all these ruins, this one was made specifically for her, disguised to look like a door reticule but only opening from her touch.

She carefully placed her palm at its center and gasped as she heard a large whoosh escape from Gaia's core as a load of pressure filed its way out. She crawled back to a standing position and watched the core moved back...and then expanded down revealing a hidden stairwell leading down into the depths of Gaia. Aloy looked at Varl and Varl looked back.

After everything stopped moving and the stairs were all in place, Varl said, "Do-do we go down?"

"We definitely go down."

He took a deep breath and followed her. As they descend, lights on the wall would flicker to life the deeper they traveled. She was surprised they still worked but this was Elisabet Sobek after all. There really wasn't much she couldn't do when it came to technology. Occasionally they would hear a slight humming noise coming from the bottom, a few seconds later it would disappear only to return and reverberate off the walls, louder and louder as they neared closer to the source.

Upon reaching the bottom they entered a large round room, completely empty except for an object in the very center and lit from the bottom of the walls to the top with that same fluorescent lighting. It cast a blue sheen on their surroundings and in a way it was familiar to the Sun Ring, albeit much less dangerous and much more clean. They also realized where the humming had been coming from.

From the center of the object, which Aloy still didn't make out, the hum emanated out from the sides, causing a shadow of light to pool on the metal ground beneath it. Each time the light would touch the floor the hum would once more vibrate throughout the room sending a dull thrum before it subsided and repeated the pattern over again.

Aloy inched closer unsure if these vibrations would harm her, she learned the hard way that ruins could be finicky in their old ways and the old ones could be strange in designing them. Varl looked on even more unsure but he didn't try to stop her.

As Aloy neared the strange object she realized that in addition to the lights, the humming, and the steady vibration she could feel through the feel, there was also a thin layer of frost radiating off its surface. It covered the panel of glass on top preventing her seeing inside. She took her hand and attempted to wipe some of it away but jerked it back immediately with a cry of pain feeling as if she'd be burned.

She grew up in the Sacred Lands where snow was practically mandatory and she had climbed mountains high enough and slick enough to give her hypothermia when she reached the top, but this was a level of cold she didn't think was possible and she looked regretfully down at her palm which was now sporting a large piece of missing flesh.

"Are you okay?" Varl asked suddenly but still keeping his distance. She had much more experience with old one ruins and technology and he didn't want to get in her way, or blow something up or essentially cause the world to self destruct again; way too much pressure, even in an empty room.

"I'm fine" she breathed, "This thing is freezing."

He inched forward slowly and examined her hand, "It took the skin right off" he said, bewildered. "Is...this, what did you call it? Cryogenics?"

"It has to be."

She stood there, motionless, her hand still burning in pain but she ignored it. This could be it, this could be her, right there in front of her but just out of reach. It was tantalizingly torturous and she had to know who was in there.

She grabbed an arrow from her quiver and began to gently scrape the frost back being careful not to crack or scratch the glass. She wasn't familiar with cryogenics, for all she knew, Elisabet would suffocate if she were opened. After a few more rakes with her metal shard, she blew the remaining frost excess away and peered inside.

A woman lay sleeping, a peaceful smile etched across her face and even from outside the stasis tube, Aloy could tell she was breathing. She dropped her arrow, for she was looking at the face of Elisabet Sobek. Alive. And now in her reach.

-3-

A voice echoed around the room, a female's voice, not entirely human but also not entirely machine. The humming stopped altogether and the room grew exponentially brighter. As if she had been waiting for the perfect moment to expose herself a thin ray of light slowly hovered down from the ceiling and came to rest gingerly in front of the stasis tube before it expanded into the familiar form and face of Gaia.

Varl's eyes widened with the same expression a deer has right before it's about to be hit by a car. He instinctively dropped to his knees in a very Lansra like fashion and pressed his forehead to the ground his arms outstretched straight ahead of him. Aloy remained still and noticed the corners of Gaia's mouth were twitching into what looked like an emphatic smile and also a mix of embarrassment.

Despite it all, Aloy wasn't really sure Gaia was aware that she was revered and worshiped by so many. More importantly, she was eternally confused as to how she was even here. Her fail safe to rid the world of Hades had brought about her own destruction, a decision she had made entirely on her own.

"How can I be of assistance?" she said smoothly before shaking her head and raising her hand at Varl in an attempt to get him standing again, "And please do not feel as if you need to bow

Varl straightened up to full attention that same look of exasperation painted on his face. How else do you act in the presence of a god? Especially one you've come to worship your entire life?

Aloy stepped forward cautiously. She had seen recordings of Gaia, conversations of her with Elisabet in the past but she was actually here this time, standing in front of her awaiting instruction. There was so much she wanted to ask and at the present moment, she couldn't think of a thing. So she asked the obvious.

"How are you...alive?" she asked for lack of a better term.

"Upon the eradication of Hades, the remnants of my core regained possession of the Spire. A lone fragment of code from Hades', the code that ciphered for the inadequacy of terra-formation passed through the remaining seven sub-functions until it found its way to me. The previous nine sub-functions are connected but are fueled independently. With Hades' code, I was able to reach out through the remaining seven to bring more of myself back online, siphoning a small amount of energy from each one to gather strength."

"But you were destroyed, I didn't think there was anything left to bring back online."

"A small piece of me remained here. A copied fragment, if you will. I no longer possess the vitality of my original design, much of it was lost in my self destruction. But, enough of me has remained here to keep watch over Dr. Sobek until someone could arrive to revive her."

"So a piece of Hades is inside you? Don't you think that's a little dangerous given all that's just happened?"

"The code is still an extension of me. Hades was created as a fail safe, should the Earth not succeed in its terra-formation, Hades would destroy everything so that I could begin anew with a different approach. However, it is the segment of code that provided the instructions for being able to indicate when that particular failure was deemed adequate enough for elimination that I now possess. The code for the elimination itself was only incorporated in Hades."

She continued, noting the confusion on Aloy's face.

"This fragment of code always belonged to me. Hades and I were connected, what one of us destroyed, the other could rejuvenate. Where one of us failed, the other would succeed. Of the nine sub-functions created, Hades and I were the closest linked, though we all shared a relationship in some small way. The Spire is our main communication relay, how we are able to extend our functions and reach across the area. After you destroyed Hades, and returned the Spire to its normal state, this shared fragment returned to me, the small fraction of me that was saved by Elisabet before she rendered herself in stasis."

"So you don't possess any of his abilities to destroy?"

"That was not my original purpose, no. I can no more destroy than Hades can create. We shared a small piece of code, that was the extent of our relationship."

"Can you be brought...back? To your original state?"

"I am unsure. I do believe it is possible though it may not be very simple. Dr. Sobek was very thorough in my design, there are things about myself even I do not know. It has been a long time since she and I have spoken. I have...missed her company."

"It sounds like you really cared about her" Aloy pondered sympathetically.

Gaia paused tentatively unsure of how to answer and after a few seconds she carefully responded with: "I was fond of her. She was my friend."

"How do I get her out?" Aloy asked nodding at the stasis tube then paused, "Does she even want to be let out?"

"It was her intention to be awakened and now that Hades is destroyed and I am somewhat functional again, I believe she would find the timing to be suitable."

"I watched the recordings. I saw what happened, how she sacrificed herself. How did she end up here? And why?"

"The probability of her fail safe had a .00001% chance of succeeding. I did not want to see her die. I convinced her to reside here, in me, and even should I somehow be destroyed, her stasis tube would be protected. This room and my core are connected, but one is not solely dependent on the other. She would feel no adverse effects from my core's...death" she hesitated, struggling to find the right term, "and she would be safe from desiccation and hindering elements."

"Even being offline, you managed to watch over her?"

"I was not entirely offline. Enough of my copied code remained to keep her alive, but that was all I was capable of achieving. With my returned fragment, I have regained some of my other functions and abilities, such as the one to appear before you now."

"So she went outside to convince everyone else that she had died? Why?"

"Because she did not want to be found. It would likely be more beneficial to you if she told you her reasons instead. I feel I do not possess the authority to define them for her. It makes me feel...unwell."

By unwell, Gaia meant guilty. She may have been created from code but Elisabet was diligent in also making her act and feel more "human". She provided Gaia with the capability to feel and extend emotion, good and bad. That included the guilt that came with discussing private matters that were not her own.

"I can assist you in bringing her out" she continued, "It is a simple process."

"Don't you wanna ask me anything first? How I got in here, for instance? I find it a little surprising that you're just going to let me waltz over there and wake her up."

"I know who you are" she affirmed with confidence, "You are the only one who can. I believe if I tried to stop you, that would displease Dr. Sobek." Aloy saw that expression return, the one edging on the brink of a smile. "You restored power to me, of which I am grateful. You also destroyed Hades, of which I am sure the world is grateful. And now you are tasked with revitalizing Dr. Sobek. I do not need to ask why. I already know. I've been waiting for this day for many days; approximately 330,000 of them.

"That long?" Varl asked, dumbfounded.

"The stasis tube keeps her body frozen in a living state.

The temperature is low enough to preserve tissue but high enough to keep blood flowing. It is like...a very long sleep."

"What do we do?" Aloy asked, ready to begin.

The humming once again thrummed throughout the room, the light once more pooling below the stasis tube before briefly disappearing. Gaia raised a hand, palm upwards, fingers outstretched and closed her eyes.

The noise of what sounded like metal grating upon metal began to grow, from a quiet hindrance to an increasing cacophony. Varl slightly winced as it began to progressively turn louder. Aloy barely flinched. After being underneath Thunderjaws, trampled by Rockcrushers and Behemoths and going face to face with the shrieking Stormbird, Shell-Walker and Glinthawk, she was surprised she could even hear at all.

As quickly as it had begun, the grating immediately stopped and the room was once more filled with silence. Gaia opened her eyes and turned to face them.

"It will only open for you" she said encouragingly, noticing the elevated heart rate in the young red head.

Aloy looked at the new addition; a console, rising up a few feet directly in front of the stasis tube with a holographic hand print glowing dully on top. Aloy slowly approached it.

"What if I never survived all this? What if I had just remained an outcast and never found her here?" she asked, surprised.

"Then she would have remained in stasis" Gaia said simply, a tone of sadness creeping in.

"You put a lot of faith in me, don't you think...?"

"Evidently, faith that was well placed. In addition, it was not I who put my faith in you" she replied, waving a hand over the stasis tube, "It was her" she finished with a small smile.

"But how could she have known?" Aloy whispered, too quiet for the others to hear.

"What are you waiting for, Aloy?" Varl smiled, "Open it."

She looked at him nervously like she was waiting for a queue or some type of permission, her hand shakily hovering over the hologram. This wasn't just anyone, this was Elisabet Sobek, the woman who was practically her mother. The entire time she was on the search for a way to destroy Hades she kept hoping she'd stumble across her, get a chance to meet her, at least touch her in some way shape or form. But those dreams were shattered when she watched that recording and now that she was actually looking at her, Aloy was terrified.

What would she think of her? Would she like her, would she be proud? Or would she be so overwhelmed and afraid that she would regret being woken up? Would she hate her for actually doing so? Her mind was a frenzy of nerves and emotions and a for a moment she forgot what it was she was supposed to be doing. She felt a reassuring hand on her shoulder and looked over at Varl who nodded encouragingly for her to proceed.

She took a deep breath and gently pressed her palm to

the console, watching the identification bars run up and down scanning her prints. After a few brief seconds, they subsided. A pause of silence. Aloy tried to steady her breathing as the frost on the stasis tube began to melt away. The sound of released pressure similar to that of the hidden entry way could be heard. Aloy moved closer, noticing a gap where the door to the stasis tube had been sealed. She gently lifted it, careful not to frighten the dazed woman inside.

Elisabet Sobek lazily stirred. Her eyes slowly opened then widened in shock and she jumped, letting out a breath of surprise at the sight of what looked like two "savages" standing over her. This caused Varl and Aloy to jump in unison.

She looked first to Varl and then set her eyes on Aloy, taking her in for the first time at a better angle. She looked at her hair, long and intricately braided but fiery like her own. Her strong round face held a band of freckles across her nose, a face that had seen much torment and much excitement, had held tears and evoked laughter, had been angry and frightened and now held her own gaze with a gentle curiosity. Her piercing hazel eyes possessed a fierce benevolence, her brows creased in worry and her hands were raised out of caution as she took a step back.

Elisabet briefly smiled and her heart raced. Could it be? She looked just like her, a younger version of her. She held the same demeanor, the same expression, the same everything. Before she could gather her thoughts to even form a sentence, Gaia's hollow voice broke the silence.

"Welcome back, Dr. Sobek. It has been a long time."

"Gaia?" she breathed, not believing it was really her.

"Hello, Elisabet" she smiled, her tone a little less formal, "How do you feel?"

Elisabet's stiffly raised a hand to her head, "I feel...very drained."

"That is normal" she reassured. "Elisabet, please remain still while I check your vitals."

She nodded, still very dazed. Aloy and Varl glanced at each other unsure of what to do or say so rather than risk spooking her a second time, they remained still and let Gaia do her work.

An ray of light emitted from Gaia's eyes and cast a sheen on the disoriented doctor as it trailed up and down her body. Aloy watched as it came in contact with her vital organs, small images of them appearing off to the side accompanied by symbols she had never seen before; numbers and percentages, some in green, others in grey, only one in yellow which was her body temperature.

Gaia retrieved the light and overall, looked rather pleased with her diagnosis; if machines can look pleased, though Aloy didn't like to think of her that way.

"Your condition is favorable" she said at last, "Your vitals look promising. Would you like to try and stand?"

"How long has it been?" she asked, ignoring the question. Gaia braced herself.

"330,000 days since stasis" she said quietly, "Which equates to approximately 903 years."

The doctor hitched her breath and fell back against the inside the tube, bracing her hands on the edges to keep herself steady. She was shivering, now not just solely because she was cold. Gaia sensed her heart rate pick up but before she could offer a solution, Aloy creeped toward her and knelt beside her.

"It's okay" she soothed gently, "Take your time."

Varl slowly unwrapped his fur coat from around his shoulders and handed it to Aloy who proceeded to wrap the doctor in its warmth. Elisabet smiled at him in thanks to which he curtly nodded and also moved closer.

"I'm sorry I startled you" she said to him, "You took me by surprise."

"Well if someone had stared at me while I was sleeping I probably would have reacted the same way."

She chuckled.

Aloy pulled the coat around her tighter ,"Is that better?" she asked.

"Much, thank you. Fingers are still a little stiff."

She kept gazing at Aloy, running between the decision of wanting to hug her but not knowing if she should, if it would be appropriate. This was as new to Aloy as it was to her, this strange being who lived centuries ago now dropped on her doorstep. But if she was able to find her and enter this room, she had to have known at least a little bit about her. Or was this all through chance and coincidence?

"What's your name?" Elisabet asked gently, never taking her eyes off her. She was afraid if she did, she might vanish into thin air.

"Aloy."

"Aloy" she repeated, feeling it for the first time on her tongue.

"This is my friend, Varl."

He raised a hand in greeting. He wondered if they realized they were practically twins and was about to point that little observation out but he decided against it and remained silent.

"I suppose you know who I am if you went through all this trouble" she said, almost guiltily.

"You're my..." Aloy wanted so badly to say mother but she stopped, "You're Doctor Sobek. Elisabet Sobek".

"It seems like only yesterday I heard that name" she answered sadly, "It's been so long."

"I'm sorry, this must be very difficult for you."

"It was my choice. I loved the world so much I wasn't ready to say goodbye to it yet and I had a very important mission that I needed to see through. I can't imagine how much things have changed since my time, hopefully not too much thanks to Apollo."

Aloy winced. Noticing this Elisabet perked up, "What?" she asked.

"Apollo was destroyed...we never learned any of its knowledge. Ted Faro. He didn't want history repeating itself, he didn't want us to make the same mistakes."

"That bastard" she growled, "He had no right to do that! He stole history and culture from you! All that work...for nothing."

"Maybe we could bring it back online, like Gaia" Aloy suggested.

"Would it matter?" Varl chimed in, "Everyone is set in their old ways, even if you put proof right in front of them, they'll never believe it. And if they do, they sure as hell won't like it."

"The Nora might not, but the Carja would be different, and the Banuk. It wouldn't just be about All Mother anymore, we could learn so much that we were meant to to begin with."

"I don't even know if it's possible. Even for me" Elisabet mused, "We had an entire team working on these sub-functions, engineered specifically for each one. It would take a long time on my own."

"You're not racing against the clock this time. You can take all the time you need, none at all if you don't want to. It's your decision" Aloy encouraged.

"One day at a time" she chuckled, "Right now, I need to see if I can stand."

She grabbed the sides of the stasis tube once more for support. Aloy stood on one side, Varl on the other to help keep her steady, their hands held out to support her in case she fell. With the help of Aloy she lifted one leg over the tube and then the other, her knees buckling as she struggled to stand.

Aloy caught her and put Elisabet's arm around her shoulder.

"Easy" she soothed.

"They say walking is like riding a bike, you never really forget. But right now I beg to differ."

Aloy glanced at Varl with a look that said what's a bike?. He shrugged and shook his head.

"You can do this. One step at a time" she smiled.

Elisabet held onto her, wincing every now and then as the blood began circulating more through her legs. She stretched one, then the other and feeling confident enough began to bend her knees.

"There you go" Aloy said excited.

She unwrapped her arm from Aloy and limped to the projection of Gaia. She raised a hand in front of her. Gaia followed suit, palm meeting palm. Human and machine, creator and creation.

"I have missed you...my friend" said Gaia despondently.

"It's only been a few seconds for me, but 900 years for you. I'm so sorry, Gaia."

"Do not be. I would never leave you Dr. Sobek. Not if I could help it. You should be aware, however, how much has changed and the events that have transpired.

I believe Aloy would be best suited to explain all of this to you. And...unless you need anything further from me, I would very much like to rest. All of my core processors and functions have gone into sustaining your life and I am...drained."

"I will fix you, Gaia. I'll put you back to normal, I promise. In the mean time, get some sleep. You deserve it."

Gaia nodded and smiled. Her projection flickered and then disappeared entirely. Elisabet side and cast her gaze to the floor, her shoulders hunched below the thick fur coat.

Aloy gently wrapped an arm around her.

"Are you alright?" she asked quietly.

"I will be. It's a lot to take in and I haven't even stepped outside yet. What is it like? Out there?"

"It's not what you remember. But, it's still beautiful...in it's own way."

"You mentioned something before. The Nora, the Carja and the...Banuk? What are they?"

"They're tribes" Aloy hesitated.

"And which one are you?"

"I'm just...Aloy" she smiled with a shrug, "Aloy despite the Nora."

Elisabet cocked her head in confusion.

42

"It's a long story."

"She's The Anointed, the all powerful head of the Nora tribe who emits bowing and praise every time someone passes her, she's practically a god, er...goddess" Varl grinned.

"Ignore him" she grumbled, rolling her eyes.

"I have to admit" Elisabet started, "I always had a plan to put myself in stasis but I never really thought about what I'd do or where I'd go when I actually got out. If I got out."

"We're way ahead of you on that. Don't worry, you'll be safe where you're going. We can talk more there, it'll be more...comfortable."

Varl edged out of the cave's opening and grimaced. "About that..." he said, turning to face them and looked specifically to Elisabet, "I don't suppose you know how to climb?"

Aloy squinted her eyes in frustration. She had completely forgotten that Elisabet wasn't exactly a brave. She would just have to override a Stormbird. If she could find one that is.

"I have an idea" she said, "but I need to go higher, all the way to the top. Look after her?"

"Of course."

The two of them moved closer to the edge, Elisabet reaching out a hand in protest before Aloy jumped from the ledge.

"Aloy, wait!" she cried. She breathed a sigh of relief as she saw a flash of red begin to shimmy up the side of the mountain. "Does she always do that?" she asked Varl.

"You get used to it" he nodded, "show off" he muttered under his breath.

The last time I was up here, this place was crawling with machines. Now that I actually want to find one, nothing. Typical.

Aloy climbed ever higher squinting her eyes from fresh snowfall as she swung from ledge to ledge, never once missing a beat. This was her element. With one hand still hanging on, she pressed her toes against the mountainside and with the other, switched on her focus.

The familiar purple map engulfed her and she looked in every direction for any outlines of machines. Luckily, there was a Stormbird perching at the top. Satisfied, she switched the focus on and continued to climb.

She sidled around to the back, out of earshot from the machine and pulled herself to the top, dropping low as she slunk to nearby foliage. The Stormbird twitched, stretching its wings before it resumed position.

Aloy crept further, quietly holding her spear. A snap on the ground caused the Stormbird to reel and turn full circle.

"Shit" Aloy groaned, realizing she had stepped on a twig. "Sorry, Rost. Guess I'm a little rusty."

The Stormbird screeched at her, it's eyes turning yellow and then red.

"Okay, guess you're still not friendly. Easy way or hard way big guy but I'm gonna need your cooperation."

In protest, the Stormbird lunged at her digging its beak into the ground, causing the mountain to vibrate in complaint.

"Hard way it is then."

Down below Varl perked up and Elisabet furrowed her brows in worry, "What is that?"

"Nothing she can't handle" he reassured her.

Aloy dodged out of the way, starting to become annoyed. She rapped her spear on the machine's side causing a component to fly loose. The Stormbird wheeled around, striking at her with its tail. She fell onto her back with a grunt, rolling to the side a split second before the bird's beak penetrated the ground a second time.

"Cut it out!" she yelled, firing an arrow into its face.

The machine staggered back on its hind legs, shaking its head before spreading its wings and taking flight.

greaaaat.

It held position in midair charging its lightning gun for attack. Aloy continued to fire, her arrows striking its weak points enough to make it flinch but not enough to knock them off. Angry, the Stormbird fired, sending an arch of lightning across the field. Aloy dodged the majority of it, but her arm was caught in the crossfire.

The impact was enough to make the mountain shake, a few stalactites falling from the ceiling.

"Oh, she's made it mad now" he chuckled.

"Shouldn't you do something?" Elisabet asked anxiously.

"She'd be angry if I did, trust me."

Aloy grunted in pain, holding her arm. She waved them both out in an arch. "Come on then!" she taunted, trying to lure the machine to the ground.

Having lost its charge, the Stormbird complied. It settled clumsily to the ground with a hop before striking out with its claws. Aloy ran and slid on her knees to its underbelly and in one swift motion pressed her spear to its core.

The machine paused, pieces of it falling off as it waited for her to finish. A few seconds later, its gaze returned to a peaceful blue and it hopped away from her awaiting instruction with a bob of its head.

"Now...how do I fly you?"

She inched closer and climbed onto its wing. It flinched in surprised but remained steady, allowing her to clamber up onto its back. She grabbed two of its wires, now a shimmering blue, and held them in a similar fashion to reins. She shook them once. The stormbird cast off from the ground and spread its wings and before too long she was soaring through air.

She steered it lower to the cave opening and noticing a lumbering machine flying straight towards them, Varl and Elisabet retreated back.

"It's okay, it's okay" Aloy reassured them as she parked it on the edge and hobbled off. "It's...friendly."

"I'm never gonna used to that" Varl exhaled.

But Elisabet was in awe. She stepped forward, gaping, and reached out a hand to touch it. The Stormbird chirped, a sound Aloy had never heard it make before. It then did something even more peculiar. It nuzzled her hand.

"That's...new" Aloy inclined.

Elisabet smiled, "Like a giant, robotic horse."

"I don't know what that is but it seems to like you" said Aloy.

"They were very majestic creatures in my time, I'm sad to see them gone."

"I've never seen a machine take to someone like that, even one that's been tamed."

"How did you manage to do that?" she asked.

"She does this thing with a spear" Varl interjected, "It's pretty cool."

"A spear? Could you show me sometime?" Elisabet asked, excited.

"I mean, it could get kind of dangerous and-"

"Aloy, I've been asleep for 900 years. I think I could use

a little adventure."

"Now you sound like Avad" she smirked.

"Who?"

"You'll meet him soon."

"Before you two stop in Meridian, mind giving me a lift back home? I think Sona will be more inclined to forgive my absence if she sees me hopping off a giant Stormbird."

"Sure, Varl."

They stopped outside the edge of Mother's Watch. Varl clambered off, immediately met by his mother who glowered at him and squinted her eyes but upon noticing Aloy perched atop, she rolled her eyes and sighed, merely pointing in the direction of the guard post and indicating for him to hurry up and just take his post.

She paid no heed to Elisabet who was still wearing Varl's coat. She held onto Aloy's waist practically hidden beneath all the fur. She tried to persuade him to take it back but he refused, assuring her that she would need it far more than he would.

Before more of the villagers could catch a glimpse or try to approach her, she urged the Stormbird back into the air and took flight for Meridian. Along the way, Elisabet would turn from side to side trying to take in the view and all who filled it, with a lot of "amazing" and "extraordinary" muttered along the way.

Aloy lightly smiled. She was glad to see this side of

Elisabet, no longer afraid but her old self: curious and imaginative, wanting to know more and drink in every ounce of knowledge and new discovery she could find. And there was so much Aloy wanted to show her.

It only took ten minutes to reach Meridian and she landed outside the gate, the cleanup crew flailing in every direction as they scrambled to get out of the way.

"Sorry!" she cried, "Still getting used to the landing."

They looked back at her, some appearing rather offended, others just grateful she hadn't taken their head off. Other still gathered around to further inspect this tame machine, jumping and retreating back every time it made a noise.

Aloy helped Elisabet down and she had come out of her coat now that the temperature had grown exponentially warmer since the mountains. She followed Aloy up the steps and through the marketplace, turning full circles, wide eyed and gaping like a child.

The sights, the sounds, the smells, they were all foreign to her. But she wanted to fully experience each one.

"Once we get you settled, you can look around as much as you want. I'll show you around myself" Aloy beamed, "Should probably get you changed first, though."

Elisabet looked down at her clothes, "Right, hadn't thought of that."

They climbed the stairs to Avad's palace. Along the way they were met with strange looks, mostly those trying to sneak a peek at Elisabet. Aloy could hear the murmur of "Never seen one of her tribe before", "Do you think she's from around here?" "She's probably a Banuk Shaman, look how strange she looks. Can never trust those ones, you know." "Looks an awful lot like that savior woman, don't you think?"

Elisabet paid none of them any attention, she was too busy taking everything in she didn't even hear them. Her face was still lit up, her smile growing wider and wider the farther up the steps they climbed. When they reached the top, they were once more met with the friendly embrace of Avad.

"Did you find me an adventure?" he smiled warmly.

Aloy motioned for Elisabet to stand beside her. "Avad, meet Doctor Elisabet Sobek. The woman who saved the plane the first time."

Avad's eyes widened, "Well now...she is quite the character."

"Dr. Sobek, meet King Avad, ruler of the Sun Carja."

"Please, just call me Avad" he continued to smile, "I hope your journey here wasn't too treacherous?"

Aloy motioned to the entryway where the Stormbird was now perching, "Not too much."

"Keep taunting me like that and one of these days I'm just going to sneak out of here and tame of those things myself."

"And then get eaten and I get thrown into jail for assisting in regicide?"

"Ye of little faith" Avad smirked, shaking his head "But, pardon my manners" he cleared his throat, "Please, let me show you where you'll be staying."

"Do you have an extra pair of clothes? Those aren't exactly of this...century" Aloy dithered.

"In the dresser. They are Carja, I hope you don't mind" he wavered to Elisabet.

"No, of course not."

"I'll let you get changed then" he said, shutting the door, before turning back to Aloy.

"Not of this century?" he repeated.

"She was frozen. In stasis."

Not catching on, Aloy used a term she knew he'd immediately understand.

"She's an Old One."

His eyebrows knitted close together in thought but he didn't protest.

"How is that possible?"

"It's called Cryogenics. Her body was frozen when she was still alive. It's like she's been asleep all this time and I've just woken her up."

"She did this deliberately?" he asked amazed.

"She said she loved the world too much to say goodbye to it and something about having an important mission she wasn't done with. When she was alive, the machine swarm practically destroyed the Earth and everything on it. The population was down to only a handful of people, but she stopped it. She found a way for life to start over, that's how we're here."

Avad fell back onto his throne in shock. Aloy was afraid it was too much for him to handle, that he would rescind his invitation to let Elisabet stay here. At the very least she was expecting him to lash out at her and tell her she was lying, that everything she just said was a complete contradiction to how he'd been raised and brought up to believe, that the Sun God was responsible for everything not Elisabet Sobek.

But all he said was, "Incredible."

"What?" she asked, puzzled.

"It's incredible" he repeated quietly, "Think of how much we could learn."

"You're not angry?"

"Why would I be angry?" he asked, astounded.

"It practically goes against everything you believe in."

"Or adds to it" he replied plaintively, "The Carja do not believe what the Nora do and the Banuk do not believe what the Carja do. All these beliefs counter-acting one another and no one is able decide which one is true. My father was a devout believer in the Sun and look what that did to his people. He was too wrapped up in his own beliefs to see that he was destroying everything around him. I don't want to be like that, Aloy" he answered sadly.

She put a hand on his shoulder, "You won't be."

They heard a door slide open behind them and Elisabet stepped out. A rich, flowing red skirt draped diagonally across her knees, held in place around her waist with a white sash. A simple white tunic covered her chest, its sleeves billowing in the wind.

"How do I look?" she asked, turning a full circle.

"Much more like you fit in" said Aloy, "How do you feel?"

"A lot better. Warmer" she nodded.

Aloy chuckled.

"Are you sure it's alright if I stay here?" She asked Avad, "I don't want to impose."

Avad taken aback responded, "My palace is your palace. Please, make yourself at home."

"Do you have a library?" she asked again.

"A what?" he looked confused.

-4-

Elisabet smiled fondly from her place on the grass. Blameless Marad had eventually managed to pull Avad away from her after what seemed like hours of conversation. He reminded the king that he was still a king and was responsible for upholding certain laws and meetings for and with the public and his discussions with Dr. Sobeck would just have to wait.

So Elisabet followed Aloy through the town, skipping the archives because she was not prepared to look through them at this point. Having spent the last twelve hours residing in the palace, being surrounded by formality with servants answering to her every whim; none of which she asked for, she was tired of being treated like Avad. Telling Aloy that Elisabet would be adequately taken care of was an understatement. She may well have been his queen and that in itelf made her extremely uncomfortable.

Not wanting to be rude, she politely informed Avad that she would very much like to accompany Aloy through the cityspace and take a breath of fresh air. The look on his face cried disappointment but he hid it with a smile as always and merely responded with "Of course, I hope I didn't overwhelm you too terribly much."

So when Aloy took her for a ride in Meridian's elevator, she not only marveled at its ingenuinity, she much more enjoyed being at the bottom, surrounded by farmland. Upon seeing grass for the first time in 900 years she immediately ran to the first clean patch she could find and stretched out on it. The sun's warmth on her face, the chattering of farmers and livestock brought a smile to her face as she closed her eyes and enjoyed the moment.

Aloy spread out beside her, raising her knees as she put her hands behind her head and stared up at the clouds. Only a few days ago that same sky looked as if it would crumble on top of them, now it was as if nothing had happend. The clean up crew however would beg to differ, they were still shifting through parts even with the help of the Oseram.

Aloy was startled out of her stupor at the feeling of something fall into her lap. Looking down she noticed she was now the proud owner of a very ragged, very dirty and torn up ball. Three children stood sheepishly at a distance. The only girl and the oldest of the pack, looking no older than seven or eight, carefully approached; the other two refusing to be left behind, afraid they'd be separated from their sister quickly followed, hanging on to her.

All three children were dressed in Carja clothing, but it was obvious they were of a lower class. Their dirty faces and tattered garb were evidence of living below the palace precinct.

"I'm sorry, miss" she had said quietly, her innocent little eyes looking to the ground with her hands behind her back like she was preparing to be scolded.

"That's okay" Aloy smiled gently and knelt beside her, handing her back the ball. The other two children stood cautiously behind her, the youngest of the three holding onto her shirt sleeve.

Noticing their apprehension, Aloy ruffled through her knapsack and pulled out an apple. "Wanna see something?" she winked.

The children hesitated but seeming a little more relaxed that she wasn't currently yelling at them like every other adult they had come across, slowly nodded their heads.

She pulled an arrow out of her quiver and held it in front of them.

"Ever seen one of these before?" she asked, wagging it back and forth between her fingers.

They shook their head, the smallest of the three now coming around from the back to stand beside his siblings, intrigued.

"Watch."

She grabbed her bow and having nocked an arrow, held it limply at her side as she tossed the apple into the air, aimed and within half a second, fired. The children's and Elisabet's eyes followed the arch. The apple fell to the ground with a thump, the arrow impaled perfectly through its center.

If the children had any remaining trepidation, it was gone now. Frowns burst into excited smiles and laughs as they clapped their hands. Aloy took a playful bow.

"You're gonna take someone's eye out with that thing!" a nearby man grumbled, adjusting his produce stall as he hovered over it protectively.

"I can handle a bow" Aloy assured him.

The three children, immediately wanting her to perform for them again rushed to the stall and each held out a coin. He handed them three apples, all they could afford, and the oldest of the batch before shaking his head in annoyance knowing exactly what they were about to do.

"Do mine first!" the middle child said, racing ahead of his siblings, apple outstretched.

Aloy pretended to sound offended. "What, only one at a time?"

The three of them all looked at each other, their eyes goggled and their mouths gaped open in smiles. Elisabet smiled warmly at their reaction. She was beginning to see Aloy, the real Aloy for how she was; not just a fearsome huntress but a tender hearted young woman. It made her own heart swell with pride.

Aloy drew another arrow and signaled for them to "fire". They threw them as high and as hard as they could, giggling all the while as Aloy judged her timing. When they had formed into a perfect arch, three arrows were let loose and pierced their targets in unison, falling neatly to the ground at their feet.

"Do it again!" the children cried, rushing back to the stall as they tried to grab another handful. This time the man's back was turned. One of the rounder Carja men Aloy had seen, his weight didn't seem at all to impair his hearing. The slightest shuffle caused him to immediately turn around, quicker than Aloy would have thought given his size, and seeing one of the children, the youngest boy, attempting to grab one of his precious oranges with his filthy hands, instantly set him in a rage.

He roughly snatched the boy's hand across the stall, yanking the orange away and holding it high out of his reach.

"No, don't do it again!" the stall owner barked, batting the children's hands away as he scowled at the young huntress. "And you! Trying to steal from me, are you!" he snapped, turning his attention back to the youngest boy; his meaty hands still holding him like a vice. His large belly pushed up against the stall making it teeter a bit on edge.

"But she's really good" the other boy pleaded, hoping that would be enough to convince him to let his poor brother go.

"I don't care if she's the queen of Meridian, I'm not running a charity here! You brats are lucky I don't skin your hides!" The oldest girl looked to Aloy despondently for help then out of habit cast her eyes to the ground as if she had given up. No adults were going to help, adults never helped. Not here.

Aloy only now realized they had given up what was

probably their week's supply of money just for a few seconds of laughter. And evidence of their first reaction to her pointed to the fact that that was a rare thing for them. And it broke her heart.

Even Elisabet began to stand at this point, but before she or his siblings could intervene or at least try and come to his rescue, the orange went sailing out of the grocer's hand with an arrow through it, piercing the tree trunk behind him. He instantly let the boy go, ducking behind his stall and covering his head. He was so large however, and his stall so much smaller, that he wasn't really doing himself any favors.

"Why don't you calm down a bit?" Aloy chided, preparing to nock another arrow as the young boy ran behind her legs and grabbed hold of one for protection.

To get her point across, she sent a second arrow a little closer to home and heard a yelp as the man tried to duck even deeper; an arrow sticking out of the tree just inches below the first one.

"I get it!" he shrieked, raising his hands in surrender. "By the Sun, stop shooting at me!"

Satisfied, Aloy set her bow down and casually strolled over to him. She reached in her pocket. He flinched before she withdrew her hand, not knowing if she was planning to torture him further but relaxed a bit when she opened a pouch of metal shards. His eyes filled with greed at the sight of them all. She flipped him one of the larger pieces, "I'll take the stall" she said confidently.

The grizzled gentlemen caught it in midair without hesitation, bit the shard to confirm its value then eyed her suspiciously, "no refunds" he warned, scratching what little of his beard was left.

She flipped him a second shard, "And that's to buy a better personality."

The man rolled his eyes and mumbled something about "Typical Nora savages...thinking they're so down to earth with their All Mother..." as he walked away.

The children gleamed with pure delight, all rushing to grab as much as they could get their little hands on, the smallest boy attempted to hoist up a watermelon, his arms immediately falling to the ground, fruit in tow, after lifting it off the stall.

"Okay, okay, one at a time. Really, this time" Aloy chuckled.

She ruffled the hair of the boy still trying in vain to lift the watermelon, his feet digging into the ground, refusing to let it be. She motioned for him to stand back and twirled her spear, sliding it nimbly between her fingers before sliding one end underneath it.

In one motion she had the fruit flying effortlessly through the air and in the next she had it sliced into three sections that landed with a soft thud on the ground. Picking up the pieces, she dusted some of the dirt off before handing a slice to each of them.

They looked at her in disbelief but beamed, their faces quickly becoming covered in juice and seeds. It wasn't often they were shown this much kindness and never had they eaten this much food in a single sitting.

Aloy knelt in front of the oldest girl and put her hands

on her shoulders. "Does someone take care of you?" she asked calmly.

"Just our mom" she said quietly.

"Take these to her" said Aloy, and removed a handful of the larger shard pieces from her pouch and put them in the girl's hand.

"I-I can't" she stammered.

"Why not?" Aloy asked gently.

"She'll think I stole them, I'll get her in trouble again."

"I think I can help with that."

After reassuring the two younger boys that yes, all of that food actually was theirs now, the three children lead Aloy to their hovel of a home. Not far away, Aloy held up a finger to Elisabet, signaling she would only be a few minutes. Elisabet smiled with a nod and proceeded to lay back on the grass and stare up at the sky again.

The three of them shifted uneasily as Aloy knocked on their door. A woman, whom she could only assume was their mother, peered out from behind it trying to hide as much of her face as she could.

"What have they done now?" she asked with dread, but Aloy could sense the sadness in her voice; the fatigue.

"Uh, nothing" she assured her.

The woman opened the door a bit wider, her eyebrows raised in shock in confusion. People only knocked on her door for two reasons: her children had caused some type of trouble or she was being charged for rent. One didn't usually accompany the other, so when a warrior woman appeared on her doorstep with her three children in tow and actually didn't have a complaint about them, she was less than mildly confused and more than pleasantly surprised.

"How-how can I help you then?" she asked, her voice hoarse from lack of sleep. Her auburn hair was streaked with bits of gray and the stress lines on her forehead made her look older than she really was. But she was altogether a rather pretty woman; her delicate face and dazzling blue eyes drew the attention away from her seemingly older age.

"I just wanted to tell you that you have three good kids and I also wanted to give you this" she said, holding a smaller pouch of shards in her hand, "They didn't want to get you in trouble."

Upon hearing this, the woman closed her eyes and smiled. Her kids weren't bad, she knew that. But they could be a handful and they knew that. When she opened them, she saw Aloy still holding the pouch out to her. She looked at the younger woman as if asking for permission and when Aloy nodded that it was okay, she carefully took it from her and opened it.

"I can't take this" she gasped, "It's too much, I'll never be able to afford enough to pay you back."

Confused, Aloy responded: "I don't want you to."

"I don't understand" she said.

"I want you to have it, no strings attached. It's a gift."

She wasn't used to gifts, especially not of this degree.

"Why? You don't even know me" she said quietly.

"No, I don't. But I've met your kids and that tells me all I need to know. So please, take it. Buy some food, pay off debts if you have any, buy some warmer clothes for the winter, whatever it helps you with."

Without a word, the woman pulled Aloy into an embrace choking back tears as she thanked her over and over again. Her husband had been killed in the onslaught against HADES and his horde of machines. He wasn't a warrior, but he enlisted himself for the battle after Erend went scouting for recruits. He had no choice. Since his death, his wife struggled to pay off the incurring debts on their home, barely making enough on her own to feed their three children and between making sure they ate, had a roof over their head and stayed out of trouble, she was nearly at her wits end.

Aloy held her tight, rubbing her back to calm her down as she continued to sob about how grateful she was. She didn't see Aloy as the "Savior" or "The Anointed" or any of the other titles people had come to refer to her as. She just saw her as a kind stranger and that's what Aloy loved most.

After wheeling the produce cart over, to which the older woman stammered over in even more disbelief, Aloy hugged them all a final time before waving goodbye and heading back to Elisabet. From the corner of her eye she could see more people look over at them, neighbors it seemed who shared in their poverty and lack of shown kindness; the elderly, the crippled, the ones most affected by the devastation. They all eyed the produce hungrily but no one dared to ask for any. The youngest boy invited them over, each handing them enough food to last for a few days. Aloy smiled at his affection.

She plopped down on the grass next to Elisabet, hands once more behind her head as she laid on her back.

"That was incredibly sweet" Elisabet said, rolling onto her side.

"I wish more people looked at me the way they just did; not a hero, not a holy figure, just...me."

"People appreciate what you've done for them. But I know exactly what you mean" she replied, sympathetic. She paused and then turned to the young huntress. "You never actually told me how you did it" she started.

"Avad didn't tell you?" the younger woman mused.

Elisabet sighed, "Avad was more interested in learning about me, about my history. I'm tired of talking about me...I want to learn more about you" she said quietly.

"I'm not that special" Aloy answered, her gaze still focused on the clouds.

"I don't believe that. From what I've actually been able to overhear, the odds were against you in every way possible and yet somehow you managed to overcome them. You did what we couldn't and you did it with just a bow and a spear." She sounded awestruck and pointing at the younger woman's weapons, continued. "That's more than special...that's...extraordinary."

Aloy seemed unimpressed, glancing momentarily at her before returning her attention upwards.

"Don't discredit yourself, Aloy."

"It wasn't just me. I had help."

"Would you tell me the story?" she asked quietly, almost pleadingly. "Please?"

Aloy turned to look at her. She could see the concern on Elisabet's face and for a brief moment she had that same despondent expression as the little girl with the ball. Elisabet was grasping at straws, battling between wanting to learn more about her daughter but not knowing if she'd like the details. She could see the scars on the young huntress's face, the battle marks that would take months to heal. She was so like Elisabet in so many ways but she was also very different; she was a warrior and part of that made her anxious. There was no telling how many times she had looked death in the eyes, but Elisabet wanted to know about all of them.

Aloy relented, "Alright" she sighed.

Aloy awoke with a start. A Carja guardsman stood over her.

"Ma'am, there are signs from the west. Sun king Avad awaits you at the temple of the Sun."

Aloy slowly nodded still overcoming the sleep. She sat on the edge of her bed as the guardsman hurried out.

'Focus. Breathe. We can beat this' she thought, beginning to strap her armor into place. She picked up her bow and slung it over her shoulder and grabbed her spear, twirling it between her fingers before sliding it behind her back. She took one final breath and headed for the temple.

'Watch over me, Elisabet. Watch over me, Rost.'

Avad was standing with his remaining guardsmen when she approached, overlooking the extant mountains of Meridian from his balcony. Smoke billowed up in the distance, rising higher and darker as the blaze of fire quickly began to spread.

"Camp fires, perhaps?" he asked hopefully, "Massing forces for the long march to the city gates?"

"That's not wood smoke."

"Then what is it?"

Aloy furrowed her brows in fear, "The end...or how it begins anyway."

An explosion erupted and Aloy and the king gasped as the mountainside began to crumble and fall. Debris and rubble sprayed through the sky like fireworks as screams and echoes of pain and terror filled the air.

Avad swallowed, his eyes filled with sadness but he did not look away.

Down the hillside Deathbringers came, accompanied by Corrupters who eagerly skittered ahead of them as if they were looking forward to the coming battle. They trudged through the grass, their lights on full alert, their guns aimed and ready to fire at whatever organic life form they could find. And there seemed to be no end to them.

"The Deathbringers you spoke of?" Avad asked with dread.

"To the guns!" shouted Aloy, ignoring him "To the guns!" she shouted motioning for his guardsmen to obey. They seemed to hesitate.

"NOW!" she barked.

"By the Sun, do as she says!" Avad snapped.

They immediately snapped to and ran down the steps to take position. The Oseram vanguard on the lower levels held fast to their guns, their armor buckling from the weight.

"All of you, be ready to fire!" the regular warned, taking up his position beside them.

"Will the guns hold them back?" asked Avad fearfully from his perch on the balcony.

"We're about to find out" Aloy replied.

But their hope was squandered as a second explosion shook the temple. Before the guards could take position, the stairwell was swept out from under them. Aloy leaned over the edge. Helis appeared below the rubble surrounded by smoke and ash; his blood red plume billowed mockingly in the wind. He jumped smoothly down to the next level, landing with a grunt as he stood tall and cocked his head. Before he could react, Helis punched the first guardsmen he saw, knocking him unconscious as his halberd fell to the ground with a clang. The others began to advance on him but Helis cut through them like air, sending two to their deaths as he knocked them off the temple.

"Helis!" Avad growled, reaching for his sword.

"No" Aloy stopped him, "Rally the vanguard and send reinforcements!"

He grabbed her arm before she could run off, "Aloy-no!" he begged.

"We need those guns" she answered, pulling away from him.

"He will cut you down!" Avad cried.

"Not this time!" she hissed before leaping over the edge.

"What was going through your head?" Elisabet asked.

"Don't die" Aloy smirked. "But mostly...just...stay focused."

"I can't imagine how you must have felt" she lauded with a shake of her head.

"I had taken Helis on once before when he locked me in a cage in Sunfall...and even once before that when he killed Rost. He wasn't getting away from me again" she growled, "I was so angry and so pent on getting revenge, I didn't feel the fear set in until after he was dead."

"Tell me more" she said gently.

"HELIS!" Aloy yelled.

Hearing her voice, the Eclipse leader turned with a sneer. His men grouped up behind him all aiming their bows in her direction. He held up a hand for them to back down. The guardsmen impaled on his sword slumped to the ground in a mangled heap as he pulled it loose.

"No. This one is mine" he smiled cruelly, slinging the blood off, "Get to the forefront, support those machines." They nodded obediently and set off down the stairs.

He puffed out his chest as he looked at Aloy, the two of them now completely alone. "I tasted his blood, you know" he mocked, "It tasted like cowardice...like failure."

Before he could say another word, Aloy had already let an arrow loose. It grazed his cheek and he laughed softly as the blood slowly began to drip down his face.

"You can't beat me, Aloy!" he beamed, his eyes alight with madness,"The Sun has chosen me!"

"Shut up and fight me!" she snapped, throwing her bow roughly to the ground as she grabbed hold of her spear.

"Gladly" he growled, his lips curling into an evil smile.

Thunder boomed in the distance and brought forth a torrent of rain. Aloy and Helis clashed, sword against spear as lightning cracked above them. Helis elbowed her in the face, his sword tip cutting deeply across her cheek as he twirled it nimbly between his fingers before slamming his foot into her midsection. She stumbled back and grunted in pain, wiping the blood away, which only made him smile even wider.

Steadying her breath she lunged forward again, sidestepping around him as he attempted to land a second blow. She dodged, rolling to the ground as he whirled around and missed her face by mere inches. Before he could counter, Aloy swiped at him from behind, managing to cut him deep on the shoulder blade before he turned and kicked her.

Her chin met his knee as he aimed upward with enough force to send her flying on her back. Her ears began to ring from the sudden force of it and her eyes went in and out of focus. He slowly walked to her as she lay on the ground, still trying to find her bearings. But before he could bring his sword down, she rolled to the side, as the blade pierced the ground.

Ears still ringing, she tried to remain focused. Her body was screaming in pain but she ignored it. Helis pulled his sword free as the rain began to pour harder, the water mixing with their blood and sweat.

They battled, clashing over and over matching each other point for point. Aloy could tell he was beginning to tire, although it was slight and she kept up her pace with him refusing to back down or show any hint of weakness or fatigue. They raged on through the storm, she couldn't tell how much time had passed.

Her breathing became more rapid but she held firm. Helis charged at her and jumped through the air, his sword aimed downward ready to strike. She struck him across the face, causing him to lose his balance as he crumpled to the ground. Not giving him a chance to regain his composure, Aloy hit him again, striking him deep through his armor, a third time with enough force to knock his sword free and a final time that managed to knock his helmet off. She was done playing games. He staggered to his feet, his breath becoming slow and raspy. She kicked him hard in the abdomen as payback and he stumbled back doubled over before falling roughly to his knees. She looked down at him, eyes full of rage as she held the tip of her spear against his heart.

"Impossible" he stuttered in disbelief "I am chosen. This was not meant to be"

Before he could say another word, she thrust it deep within his chest. He sputtered, his cold eyes staring at her in contempt, his mouth gaped open in shock and pain.

"Chosen? HADES only chose you because you're a fool. A sadistic butcher too stupid to see you were being used" she growled, twisting the spear even deeper. "Your whole life was a failure and soon, no one will even remember you. Turn your face to the Sun and think about that!" she spat, yanking it free. He sputtered a final time before falling to the ground in defeat.

Elisabet looked at the younger woman's face, the gash she had received from Helis was deep. It spread out from the bridge of her nose and although no longer bleeding, it would take many weeks to heal. It made her heart ache knowing Aloy had felt pain, that this sadistic monster had harmed her daughter even if she hadn't seen her in nineteen years. Aloy noticed her brows furrow in anger as she looked at her scar.

"It doesn't hurt anymore" she assured her. She pointed to it, "This is nothing."

But she was proud of her, proud of this young woman who battled the leader of an entire army single handed and came out victorious.

"You could have been killed."

"If I had a shard for every time that's almost happened..."

Elisabet eyed her knowingly, not giving away how concerned that made her feel.

"What happened next?"

With Helis finally dead, Aloy leaped from the temple and rode the zip line down to the forefront of the battle at the city gates.

The Oseram vanguard had managed to so far hold the machines back but where one became destroyed, two more popped up in their place.

The sound of rockets whizzed through the air from the Deathbringer's guns before ending in an explosion at the city's sealed gates.

"Where do you need me?" Aloy shouted above the noise.

"Take up a cannon, on the platforms!" Petra cried, firing off another round.

At least ten Deathbringers loomed in the distance surrounded by other, smaller machines. They were slow but they were powerful and they weren't holding back.

Aloy's body shook as she fired the cannon, sending an arch of explosives to the nearest Deathbringer she saw. It wasn't phased, continuing to march forward. Corrupters spiraled out from behind them as they rushed ahead to cause even more damage.

From her platform Petra fired again, managing to bring one down before she stopped to reload.

Petra was accompanied by four of her fellow Oseram all in possession of a cannon but it wasn't enough to stave off the attacks. The machines just kept edging closer the harder they fought back.

"Keep firing, Aloy!" a female's voice called, "We'll distract them!"

Aloy turned to see Vanasha and Uthid charging forward, spears at the ready as they rushed into the fray.

"Vanasha, wait!" Aloy cried.

Vanasha never stopped running but merely turned her head back with a smile and saluted before disappearing into a cloud of smoke; Uthid right behind her.

The Oseram kept up their charge, firing round after round at Petra's command. Three Deathbringer's fell, two corrupters followed suit. The smaller machines were beginning to near closer and Aloy could see a Bellowback among them.

She was trying her best to damage the machines near Vanasha to at least weaken them enough for her to pick them off. Vanasha slid under the Bellowback, cutting it down the middle of its gullet with her spear.

The Oseram archers finished it off. A second one turned on its hind legs, sending forth a wave of fire. Vanasha pushed Uthid out of the way, catching it full force before the machine charged into her.

She crumpled to the ground. She attempted to get up but her arms gave way as she tried to lift herself. Enraged, Uthid charged forward, stabbing the Bellowback in its cargo sac. It exploded, the blaze it carried leaking out onto Uthid's hands. He gritted his teeth through the pain but only dug his spear even deeper sending the machine to its mechanical grave.

Aloy fired at the third one causing it to stumble back while Uthid gathered Vanasha in his arms and carried her off the field.

Talanah and her hunters met them midway sending a storm of arrows at the machines that followed them. A Stormbird and three Glinthawks flew ahead, eyes only for Aloy. Petra turned and fired at them, sending two of the hawks to the ground in a burning heap before the Stormbird fired its lightning at her.

Petra dove out of the way, more nimble than she looked and held fast to her gun. Aloy fired in unison, the Stormbird angered at her interference. It swooped down and dove at her, claws outstretched. Aloy ducked beneath it and fired again, hitting it square in its jet engines. It fell to the ground no longer able to fly and charged at her with its beak.

Before Aloy could fire a third round, Petra beat her to it hitting the machine full force in the face before it sputtered in a cloud of smoke. Aloy nodded her thanks.

Time passed slowly but the Deathbringers kept coming.

Most of the vanguard managed to beat back the other machines but the Deathbringers were difficult to bring down and more kept appearing over the horizon pent on breaking through the city gates.

Those holding the front line began to retreat as the machines slowly pushed them back. Aloy ran to Vanasha and Uthid. He was ducked behind one of the platforms holding her in his arms. Her body was blistered but she just smiled up at him. "Look what you made me do" she chided weakly, holding up her arm. "This skin is gonna look like leather when it heals."

He dropped his head and sighed in annoyance, "Save your strength, woman. Quit talking so much."

Her laugh turned into a cough as she replied, "That's the thanks I get for saving your sorry hide?"

"You shouldn't have moved" he said, guilty.

She held a hand to his face, "I wasn't about to let that pretty face of yours get all burnt up."

Aloy knelt beside them.

"There she is" Vanasha coughed, "The woman of the hour."

"Is she okay?" Aloy asked him worriedly.

"She's fine" Vanasha answered before he could reply. He looked at her disapprovingly.

"What did I just say?"

She waved him off.

"Find Teb" Aloy told him, "He'll know what to do." She got up to leave but Vanasha stopped her.

"I don't think it'll matter much longer" said Uthid sadly, looking at the onslaught of Deathbringers. "But at least we tried."

"This isn't over" said Aloy, "Not yet."

"Where are you going?" Vanasha winced.

"To finish this."

Uthid nodded, "Go, I'll take care of her."

"Aloy" she called again. Aloy turned. "If you die...I'll kill you."

Aloy sighed with a smile and nodded before grabbing her bow and rejoining the vanguard at the gate. From the corner of her eye she could see one of the Deathbringers aim. Seconds later it fired, sending a hail of rockets directly at the gateway doors.

"Incoming!" Aloy yelled.

Before she could move, the rockets landed on the arch above her. She shielded her head as the rubble fell on top of her and everything went black.

...

...

A Deathbringer marched through the opening. Dragging behind its rear was the core of HADES, emanating with tendrils of red corruption.

Aloy stirred. Smoke burned her eyes and she looked to the sky seeing nothing but red. This was it. The end was here. She had to get up, had to keep going but her body wouldn't let her and she crumpled back to the ground.

She felt a hand on her shoulder and a voice called her name.

"Aloy!" he cried.

She tried to move, cringing as she felt her ribs. The same voice began to gently shake her, and she could hear the panic in his tone.

"Aloy!" he tried again, "Aloy!"

She opened her eyes blinking until the figure crouched in front of her became focused. He looked down at her with worried eyes but he also looked relieved that she was alive.

"Teb...?" she asked weakly as he took her hand and helped her to her feet.

"By All Mother, you survived" he breathed a sigh of relief, "I thought you were killed."

"The others...are they...?" she asked fearfully.

"No" he quickly reassured her, "No. Wounded, but alive, mostly. The machines blasted through and kept going. They marched on the Spire dragging that...thing with them."

Aloy nodded and looked in the direction he was pointing then put a hand on his shoulder, "Take care of the others, Teb. I've got to go."

Behind her there was nothing but rubble, ahead of her there was nothing but destruction. Everything was in flames. People ran about trying in vain to put some of them out, others lay moaning on the ground in pain. Some didn't move at all.

She wanted to stay and help, at least see if her friends were okay but she couldn't. She ignored the wreckage and chaos around her and just ran. Her body was screaming, her muscles were on fire and in all her nineteen years she had never pushed herself this hard or this fast. But she blocked it out and kept going.

Miles down the road to the temple itself, ledge after ledge that she pulled herself up and higher to the top with her ribs feeling like they had snapped into a dozen pieces, and even higher still as she darted up the stairs that hadn't totally been destroyed.

But HADES had beat her to the top and was uploading his signal to the Spire's base. A red aura emanated from it's tip, surrounding the entire city of Meridian in its evil glow. And it would bring every machine, no matter how old or long buried and forgotten, back to life.

The fact that she was seeing this signal meant that Erend's vanguard had failed. She only hoped he was still alive. Sona, Varl, they were up there too.

She grit her teeth and kept running, jumping over the gaps HADES had caused as she worked her way to the top.

"Gotta keep going" she grunted, pulling herself up and over another ledge, "Gotta keep pushing...knew this wouldn't be easy."

-5-

"So...Free Heap...?"

"What about it?" Aloy asked, arching an eyebrow.

"Will you take me?"

Aloy rubbed the back of her neck with apprehension and sighed, "I suppose."

"What's the problem?" Elisabet asked, noting the young huntress's concern.

"Well, safety for one thing. You aren't exactly an aspiring warrior" Aloy replied, pointing at the older woman's civilian garb.

Elisabet scoffed with a smirk, "I'm sorry, I didn't have time to become an expert huntress. I was too busy trying to save the world."

Aloy relented, "You know what I mean" she answered apologetically.

"Then teach me" she said simply.

"What?" Aloy asked flatly.

"Teach me to fight, teach me how to protect myself."

Aloy backed up with her hands raised but Elisabet merely followed her forward.

"I'm not exactly teacher material" Aloy hesitated, trying to come up with an excuse as she continued to back up but Elisabet wasn't going to budge.

"I'm sure you'll do fine" she defended, as Aloy finally backed herself up against a tree, "I'm a quick learner. Besides, I can always try and teach myself but I think we both know how that would end up. I can see it now, me shooting an arrow that happens to hit a Thunderjaw and then that Thunderjaw uproariously charging at me and right before it eats me for dinner, I would think to myself: 'If only Aloy would have properly taught me how to use this thing, maybe I would have survived.'"

Aloy sagged her shoulders with another sigh, "Fine", she glared, "I'll teach you."

Elisabet smiled and patted her on the cheek.

Aloy pointed a stern finger at her before relinquishing her position at the tree, "but no firing at anything, least of all a Thunderjaw."

"Deal."

The two of them set off for free Free Heap that next morning, taking flight on the friendly Stormbird that had patiently and loyally waited for them outside the city gates. It had covered itself beneath its massive wings and was exuding a high metallic chirping noise that Aloy could only assume was meant to be snoring. The various denizens of Meridian would sometimes approach it with apprehension, which was understandable, but when they understood that the large machine was in fact docile and meant them no harm, many would often bring food for it in the form of whatever they had available, or more likely, whatever they didn't want or could no longer use. Nevertheless, the Stormbird seemed appreciative and after finishing its meal, would then continue its slumber.

Aloy placed her hand gently on the bird's back then slowly retreated as it began to stir and uncurled its body. Elisabet watched in awe as the Stormbird stood to its full grandeur, but not before stretching each of its legs. With a shake of its wings and head, it turned to the two women and instinctively lowered itself, allowing the two of them to clamber onto its back.

"I think you've found yourself a pet, Aloy" the older woman mused, wrapping her arms around her daughter's waist as the young huntress adjusted position.

"Did your dog ever try to kill you?"

"No, can't say he did."

"Then I don't think this constitutes as a pet" Aloy smirked.

The Stormbird chirped in response before taking a running start and ascending into the air. After a few moments, it had become accustomed once more to flight and began to glide effortlessly through the air only stopping to occasionally flap its wings.

"I think you should give it a name" said Elisabet, after things had quieted down.

"What is it with you and naming things?"

"Humor me."

"Alright, how about 'machine'?" she answered sarcastically.

Elisabet lightly smacked her on the shoulder, "I said humor me"

"You know these things don't respond to names, right?" she asked.

"Have you ever tried calling one by a name?"

"Yes, usually by 'uh oh' or 'this isn't good' or even the occasional 'oh shit', but I think my favorite is probably 'that's gonna leave a mark in the morning'."

"Oh, har har" Elisabet mocked. In front of her, Aloy smirked as she was met by another light smack.

"You're good at names, you do it."

"I had a dog named Robo, do we really want to get into this again?"

"Humor me" Aloy teased, glancing over her shoulder.

"You tamed it, you get the honor of naming it."

"I already suggested machine and you shot it down."

"That's too impersonal...and too obvious."

"Fine, fine. How about...bird?"

"You're terrible at this."

"I don't see you giving me any ideas" Aloy grumbled

"It would be helpful to know what sex it is"

"I...don't think that's a thing with these."

"It is. Ted was very...thorough... in his designs."

"Why?"

"It's Ted, do you really need to ask?"

"How would you...check for that? Because I'm not sticking my hand anywhere near...that" Aloy grimaced.

"I suppose like anything else. I'll do it when we land, I'm curious now."

"You go right ahead" Aloy muttered.

The flight to Free Heap was a relatively calm one and for a while, the two of them rode in silence simply enjoying the scenery and fresh air. Despite growing up in the outdoors among the frigid landscape with the Nora, or rather lack thereof, Aloy would always find comfort in nature and there was something freeing about being up in the air away from the crowded cities and people who always wanted her attention. She was in the one place they would never be able to reach her. Elisabet sat quietly behind her, looking out over the countryside. The change did not sadden her, but it was not altogether welcoming and she clung tighter to Aloy as the only familiarity that she currently had.

They stopped in a clearing near a small stream for a time to stretch. Normally Aloy would have kept going, distance didn't usually bother her as she was used to rougher terrain and longer periods of travel. Being hunted usually achieved little break time. But for Elisabet's sake, though she never complained, Aloy ordered the Stormbird to land.

"Why are we stopping?" Elisabet asked as Aloy hopped down from its back.

"Figured you could use a break" she shrugged, throwing her pack to the ground.

"I'm old, but I'm not that old" she teased.

"You're sassy today" Aloy playfully chided.

"I seem to recall you once telling me that you were the 'hardest of the asses', where do you think you get it from?" she smiled.

As soon as the words left her mouth, Elisabet wondered if she shouldn't have said them. Was that too soon? Her smile began to slowly fade; Aloy could be hard to read at times, another gift she had passed onto her. But Aloy was also curious like herself and she cocked her head at Elisabet and chuckled causing the smile to once more return.

"I think..." Aloy began, picking up her bow, "that it's a perfect time for you to practice with one of these."

"Really?" Elisabet's eyes lit up as she strode to her daughter. Aloy nodded and held it out for her. Elisabet eyed it before looking up at her but when Aloy nodded with a smile, she carefully took it from her and held it as if it were made of glass.

"You won't break it" she said, amused, "trust me."

"But it's your bow. I was expecting some cheap beginner's bow, what if I...do something to it?" she asked with trepidation.

"It's just a bow" she assured her, "You'll be fine."

Elisabet sighed and nodded as Aloy stepped in behind her. She positioned the bow between Elisabet's hands, lightly drawing her into a proper stance before stepping off to the side, "Fingers here and here" she said gently pointing at the strings as Elisabet followed suit.

"Good, now wait there."

Aloy rummaged in her pack and drew out an apple and using a few rocks beside the stream bed, stacked them together to form a makeshift pedestal. Placing the apple on top, she resumed her position beside her mother.

"I'm starting to wonder if you have a vendetta against fruit" the older woman joked.

"I pulled a tooth out on of these things when I was a kid, never forgave them for that" she answered simply.

From the quiver she always kept on her back, Aloy proceeded to pull an arrow from it and handed it to Elisabet who proceeded to nock it without much difficulty.

"Not bad. Now, just pull it back."

Elisabet's arms shook at the bow's give and Aloy covered her mouth to stifle a giggle. After a few seconds, she finally managed to pull it all the way back and looked to Aloy for further instruction.

"Let go" she nodded, placing her hands on her knees as she knelt down to watch.

Elisabet drew a breath and focused her sights on the apple, not blinking, not even breathing. She let the arrow fly watching her target all the while. But, the apple stayed where it would and the arrow flew far left of its mark and pierced the ground behind it. Elisabet cocked her head and pouted before turning back to her daughter for her input.

"It takes practice, no hunter or huntress for that matter ever became an expert in a day."

"But you will teach me?"

"I will teach you" she affirmed, "but you're going to need a lot more than just bow practice. We have to build your upper body strength first. Rost wouldn't even let me touch a bow until he knew I could pull the strings back without give. It won't be easy, but if you want to learn, I'll teach you all I know."

Elisabet nodded and smiled before handing her back the bow with a genuine "Thank you."

Before stowing it behind her shoulder in its normal location, Aloy frowned at the apple and after retrieving her arrow from the ground, sent it flying straight through the fruit's core and caused it to repel off its pedestal with a soft thud. Elisabet eyed her quizzically.

"I hate apples" she shrugged, before pulling her arrow free.

Rather than continue their flight to Free Heap, Elisabet suggested they camp out instead. Evening would be upon them in a few hours and she hadn't seen the night sky lit up with stars since her days on the farm, of which there were few and far between of as she got older. Aloy was all too happy to agree, sleeping under a roof wasn't the norm for her. So the young huntress busied herself with unloading her gear as the Stormbird stayed faithfully by her side, all the while watching her intently as she began to set up camp.

"I gotta ask..." Aloy began, unraveling two bed rolls, "Why do you want to learn all this stuff? Don't get me wrong, I have no qualms about teaching you, but there are plenty of people who don't know how to fight or hunt or do any of the things I do and they get along fine."

Elisabet pondered, thinking carefully about how to respond as she set an armful of firewood down. 'Because you're my daughter and this is the only way I know how to relate to you' she thought, then shook said thought away before answering with, "Well if there's another cataclysmic event that happens on this poor planet, at least I'll know how to properly defend myself this time instead of hiding away in a bunker." She said it jokingly, but she meant it.

Aloy looked taken aback, "You weren't hiding, you were helping."

"I was locked away in safety while everyone on the outside kept throwing themselves at those damn machines just to buy me time for a weapon they believed would save everyone...a weapon that would never come. It never existed but I still feel like I failed them."

Elisabet closed her eyes and sighed, trying to fight back the anger and sadness. Aloy placed a gentle hand on her shoulder and Elisabet looked into her daughter's eyes.

"It's not your fault" she said quietly, "You did everything you could and there's honor in that."

Elisabet pulled away from her more sharply than she had intended, "I stood in the ashes of a billion souls and asked the ghosts if honor mattered" she glowered, "The silence was my answer."

Aloy opened her mouth to speak but had no words to say.

"I didn't do enough" Elisabet whispered, more to herself than Aloy, "I would have done anything to save them."

Aloy knelt beside her, "I know" she nodded.

Elisabet looked up at her, her eyes watering. "I"m sorry, I didn't mean to- I-"

Without hesitation, Aloy pulled her into a hug. She was surprised by her own affection but something about it just felt...right. She had unfrozen this woman from a 900 year slumber, introduced her to an entirely different world with entirely different rules with nothing and no one that was familiar to her out of the selfish need for some type of motherly figure that she wasn't even sure Elisabet wanted. And now it was all crashing down on her, it was all becoming real, and it was a lot for her to handle.

Aloy wrapped her arms tightly around her and Elisabet

blinked in surprise, forgetting her sadness for a few seconds. And as Aloy held on tighter, refusing to let go, Elisabet slowly brought her arms up as well and clasped them around her daughter squeezing her eyes shut as she gripped her tighter, trying to fight back tears. Aloy could feel her body clench as she held them back, refusing to let her guard down, refusing to appear weak. In her time, she was used to being a leader, a figure that people looked to for answers and for hope. She staved off the fear that kept everyone else around her bolted down. Back then she had only been filled with rage, the only thing she could turn to to keep that same fear hidden. It was more than just saving those on the outside, it was about destroying the things that had caused them so much pain and it was only enhanced by the realization that she couldn't do a damn thing to help them.

But now? Now there was only sorrow and it was hitting her all at once.

"It's okay" Aloy soothed.

Such simple words, but enough to break her barrier. She couldn't hold it back anymore and Aloy held her tight as her body wracked with sobs. Elisabet clung to her, the only semblance of her past life she still had left. But for now, it was enough.

Aloy remained where she was as Elisabet began to slow her breathing back down to normal. She gently pulled away from her and sniffed, wiping stray tears from her eyes.

"I'm sorry" she said, sounding embarrassed. Or was it shame?

"You don't have anything to be sorry for. I understand what it's like to want to save someone that you can't."

" I shouldn't have taken it out on you, either."

"I've been told worse" she lightly smiled.

"It's just- it's a lot. I should have expected to feel overwhelmed by now but-"

Aloy held up a hand, "I know" she assured her, "If anything, I should be the one apologizing. I didn't stop to think whether you'd actually want to be woken up. I'm sorry I never...asked is the wrong word, but-"

"No" Elisabet said, cutting her off, "I wanted to. I was meant to. I had a mission...have a mission and I have to see it through."

"What is it?"

"It's extremely important to me"

"You can't tell me?" she asked trying not to sound hurt.

"Not right now" she said quietly, "Please understand."

"I do."

"I will one day when I've seen it through, I promise."

"Alright. Let me know if I can do anything to help."

Elisabet smiled, "You already have."

It was less of a mission and more of a journey.

Year 2064

"Elisabet are you positive you want to proceed?"

"Yes, GAIA. This is something I know in my heart I have to do."

"But you risk the possibility of never waking up."

"I know. But I also know you and I trust you."

GAIA looked at her sadly and pursed her lips as Elisabet walked to her and held up her palm. GAIA followed in her direction and there they stood saying their last goodbyes in silence.

"Elisabet-"

"I'll be fine, GAIA. And if I'm not...then it wasn't meant to be."

"You are placing a high amount of trust in an individual who does not yet even exist. The probability is-"

She gently broke her off, "The probability doesn't matter" she answered softly.

"But you could die" the sorrow in her voice creeping in.

Elisabet smiled, "I'm going to die anyway, whether it's out there or in here. At least through this, I might get the chance to meet her. And if I don't, if she doesn't find me, if she...can't...then I'll never know and I'll be none the wiser."

"If you are sure"

"I am."

"Then have finished preparations" she said quietly, "only your genetic construct will be able to open this door."

"Not my genetic construct, more than that" she said proudly.

GAIA paused, trying to find her words carefully and Elisabet could see her searching her data banks for the correct term, "Your...daughter...will only be able to open this door."

Elisabet smiled instantly, "Daughter" she murmured, the word strange on her tongue, "I always wanted a daughter."

She began lowering herself in the stasis tube and GAIA sensed her heart rate picking up, her nerves become tangled. Trying to comfort her in the best way she knew how, she stayed on topic and asked her: "What would you want her to be like?"

Elisabet swallowed trying to steady her breathing, "I would want her to be curious...willful...and compassionate" she finished softly.

"That is not unlike yourself."

"She won't be exactly like me and I don't want her to be. She's her own person."

"Your DNA will be in her, she will not be completely identical" GAIA paused a second time before saying, "But she will be yours."

Elisabet quickly wiped a stray tear away before fully laying down. GAIA looked to her for approval and when she nodded to proceed, GAIA closed her eyes. The tube's lid began to slowly lower itself, sealing her in with a hiss as she tried to remain calm. A few seconds later she could feel her body grow tired and her eyes struggled to stay open as her skin began to grow cold. The feeling reminded her of a deep anesthetic and she could no longer fight it off. Her breathing returned to normal and her vitals, to GAIA's standards, were level.

In the sealed chamber of Thebes, the last known bunker of humankind, Elisabet lay in silence. GAIA kept watch, shutting down her non critical functions before joining her in a deep sleep of constant vigil. And for the 903 years she would remain there keeping guard over the woman who had given her life, she would stay loyally by her side.

They camped under the stars that night and for the first time in a long time, Elisabet finally felt at ease. The sky looked no different than it had during her childhood, even though she knew it bore scars that would likely never heal. Aloy had long past fallen asleep and Elisabet smiled over at her every time she twitched or made little huffs of breath in her sleep. Beside them, the Stormbird could be heard resuming its metallic snoring beneath its wings. Between the sights and sounds, Elisabet felt like she was back home on the farm. She could carve out a life here, it wouldn't be the same, but that didn't have to be a bad thing.

...

...

Aloy awoke that morning to the sounds of more metallic

chirping. She opened one eye. Elisabet was stroking the Stormbird, rubbing the side of its face like a horse and though it was the complete opposite, it seemed to enjoy it. It was even a bit taken aback when the older woman stopped and nudged her hand for her to continue.

"I think it would be safer to say that you have a pet" Aloy yawned, stretching her arms to the sky, "That thing likes you far more than it likes it me."

"Maybe because I give it attention" she playfully scolded.

"I stuck a spear in its back, I don't think it wants anymore attention from me."

"Speaking of which, I think it's time we figure out what we're working with here. Come here."

Aloy eyed her with suspicion, "Why?"

"Just come over here" she repeated.

Aloy did as she was told.

"While I've got it relaxed, look beneath and see what sex it is."

Aloy frowned at her.

"Aren't you curious even in the slightest? Yesterday you didn't even know they had a sex."

Aloy blinked and continued to frown, unfazed.

"If you won't, I will."

At that she sighed and held up a hand for her not to move. Aloy had a lot more experience with these machines. She also didn't want Elisabet to get hurt and no matter how friendly this Stormbird appeared to be now that it was docile, Aloy still treated it with caution. She had been in her fair share of scrimmages with them to know what they were capable of and more importantly to never fully trust one even if it was tamed.

Aloy knelt beside it and looked up underneath, "What exactly am I supposed to be looking for?"

"I guess if you see anything dangling, you'll know."

"Lovely..."

After a few quick peaks from a few different angles, Aloy resigned in her inspections. She had fought machines, destroyed machines, even tamed machines, but sexing a machine was something she never thought she'd be adding to her list. There really wasn't that much to see except a slight indent made of a slightly different shade of metal where one would expect such appendages to be.

"Well?" Elisabet asked when Aloy had finished.

"Well I didn't see anything...obvious..." she paused.

"Well then, it looks like we can stop calling it 'it' and start calling her, 'she'"

"If you say so" Aloy shrugged.

"I thought of a name, by the way. I stayed up last night looking at the stars, thinking back to my time in college.

I took a class in world religions once in my early years there. Christianity, Hinduism, Buddhism, many religions in my time were at an end. But to learn of so many beliefs and thought processes from different cultures always fascinated me. My professor once spoke of a Hindu god associated with storms and lightning. I believe it's fitting considering our friend here" she said, patting it on the beak.

"What was the god's name?"

"Indra."

"I like it."

"Then Indra it is."

They arrived in Free Heap that afternoon although the war had taken its toll on many aspects Free Heap was a strong and formidable village and the Oseram who called it home were even stronger. Bred from iron and steel, the Oseram had rebuilt that which was broken in a matter of days and Free Heap looked no worse for wear. On the contrary, under Petra's command, it seemed even more sound and sturdy than it had before. Around the exterior of the village, there was now a wall of concrete and stone that stretched all the way down to the river bed and surrounded Free Heap on every side. It was no longer open to public access and was under constant surveillance by numerous Oseram guards who patrolled its border. On each corner of the wall erupted a guard tower and housed in each tower was a mounted cannon. Aloy shuddered at the thought of having to use one of them again. The last few times had nearly dislocated her shoulder.

Aloy flew over the wall's confines and landed in an

open area away from most of the public, though the sudden appearance of a giant Stormbird clanking to a halt, like the Carja, sent a majority of the Oseram scurrying in a different direction. A few remained behind with their halberds raised, but upon realizing that Aloy was controlling it, they immediately lowered them and proceeded to wave at her with smiles.

"Stay here...Indra" said Aloy, the idea of calling a machine by a name would take some getting used to. Indra chirped in response, though whether it was because she understood she was being talked to or it was out of habit, Aloy didn't know. Before she could take two steps she was lifted into the air by Erend who proceeded to sling her over his shoulder and spin around a few times before setting her back down.

"Aloy!" he cried, holding her out at arms length, his hands on both her shoulders, "You're here! How are are you!"

"I'm good, Erend" she chuckled as he shook her roughly with his excitement, "How are things?"

"Good, good. Take a look around, we've done a lot of remodeling" he said motioning at the wall.

"I saw, it's a nice touch."

"If it keeps the damn Eclipse out, it'll be more than that."

"You're still having problems with them?"

"No, they haven't showed their sorry hides since you destroyed HADES but I'm sure there's still a few stragglers around somewhere. Course, it helps with the raiders and Glinthawks too but they haven't been around in awhile either. Not that I'm complaining, mind you."

Erend caught sight Elisabet out of the corner of his eye. She was standing cautiously behind Aloy. He looked to Elisabet then to Aloy then back to Elisabet then back to Aloy again before taking a step back to reassess what he was seeing.

"Either I drank a lot more ale than I thought I did or I'm going crazy, because either is possible, but I'm seeing two of you."

"It's a long story" said Aloy as she gently pulled the older woman in front of her, "This is Dr. Elisabet Sobeck. Dr. Sobeck, this is my good friend, Erend."

Erend bowed politely in front of her before extending his hand, "Any friend of Aloy's is a friend of mine."

Elisabet shook his hand and smiled, "It's nice to meet you, I've heard stories about you."

"Well that's a scary thought" he chuckled, "hopefully they weren't too traumatizing."

"She told me how you helped defeat HADES, it was very brave."

"Ahh, that was all Aloy. We were mainly the distraction" he said with a wave of his hand.

"Don't sell yourself short, Erend. I couldn't have done it without you" she said patting him on the shoulder.

"Well, thanks. Glad I could help" he nodded with a smile.

"Is Petra around? I got her letter, she said she had something for me."

"Yeah, she's over at the forge. Go on over, I'll catch up with you later. I just remembered something I have to do, but I expect a drink from you before you leave. I still owe you for helping me with Ersa."

"You paid me back with HADES."

"Well then I owe you for keeping me alive" he suggested, "Just have a drink with me."

"Alright, alright."

He smiled at them both before running to catch up with his fellow guardsmen. Aloy motioned for Elisabet to follow as they walked upstairs to Petra's forge. As per usual she was busy working on it, though what she was possibly conjuring up this time, Aloy wasn't sure she wanted to know. In her letter, Petra had assured her that her new toy was less dangerous, but her definition of dangerous and Aloy's definition of dangerous were entirely different.

"Petra?" Aloy called, not wanting to disturb her. Petra turned and grinned and then immediately looked confused.

"Damn...they must have spiked that ale hard today."

"You're not seeing double, she's real."

"No kidding?" she gaped, looking Elisabet up and down before reaching out to poke her on the forehead, causing the older woman to jump, "Well, damn. You two are practically twins. Is this your long lost sister or something because honestly, nothing surprises me around here anymore."

"Uhh...something like that" Aloy stammered.

"You got a name or am I gonna have to call you Aloy two?" she asked.

"Elisabet...Lis" she answered.

"Well, hello, Lis. You can call me Petra."

"And as for you" she said, turning back to Aloy, "I see you got my letter."

"Yes, it crashed through my window one night while I was asleep" she frowned.

"Agh, sorry, I had to use one of the stupid ones. All my good messenger geese were in use."

"You trained a goose to carry messages?" Lis asked.

"Well I figure if Aloy can train a machine, I could train a goose. Though, it would probably be a lot easier if my hunters would stop eating them" she said with annoyance, "At least you got my message, didn't think it would get to you. I have a new toy for you."

"So I hear."

"Now. I know what you're thinking-"

"Will it explode?" she asked sternly.

"Define 'explode'"

100

"Petra..."

"It won't explode...per se."

"Per se?"

"Wait here."

Petra strode behind her forge and began rummaging through a bin of her previous inventions. She was completely hidden from view but every now and then Aloy would see her throw something over her shoulder. It would soar through the air before landing harshly on the ground. After about three or four of her "toys" found themselves on the ground, Petra returned. She twirled an arrow between her fingers and handed it to Aloy, "Know what that is?" she asked.

"...I would hope" the huntress replied.

"Prototype design, think I finally got all the kinks out."

"What does it do?"

"I'll show you. KAELUF, COME HERE!"

Lis and Aloy jumped as Petra called over the forge's edge. A few moments later, Kaeluf slumped up the stairs and sighed, "Please tell me you aren't gonna-" he began, too quiet for anyone to hear.

"Just the man I was looking for" Petra grinned, wrapping her arm roughly around his shoulder, "I need you to test out my arrow again."

He closed his eyes and grimaced, "I still haven't got

feeling back in my-"

"I aimed a bit low that time, I'm sorry, but I worked all the kinks out this time. Should work like a charm."

"You said that last time" he groaned.

"And last time I was right. Those were old kinks, these are new ones."

"Can't you ask Rasgrund to do it?"

"Rasgrund didn't run off in the middle of the night, shirking his guard duties to go drinking, now did he?"

"It was one time!"

"Two times! You think I don't know everything that goes on around here? Now go stand over there and hush."

He sagged forward and did as commanded as Petra motioned for Aloy to draw her bow. She hesitantly nocked the arrow and looked at Petra with dread, but Petra merely looked at Kaeluf and sweetly smiled before saying to Aloy "Go ahead, shoot him."

"Wait-what?" she asked.

"You won't hurt him" she dismissed, waving her hands.

"Nothing except my pride" he groaned.

"Zip it!"

"Petra..."

"I've tested it on him before, he'll be fiiiiine."

"You shot him with an arrow?" she asked sternly.

"Only twice."

"It's fine, Aloy", sighed Kaeluf, "They only-"

"Don't tell her, you'll ruin the surprise!"

"Just do it" he winced, covering his groin.

Aloy hesitated but Petra kept nodding for her to continue. Finally she fired it but rather than piercing his skin, the tip of the arrow that Aloy hadn't realized had actually been coated in rubber, let out a tremendous jolt of electricity that caused Kaeluf to seize up and fall back in paralysis.

"YES!" Petra cheered, "Finally got that damn thing to work right!"

"Kaeluf, are you okay!" Aloy cried as Lis covered her mouth.

"He's fine!" she answered for him as he held up a shaky thumbs up before allowing his arm to fall back to the ground, "Though he probably won't be moving much for the next 24 hours."

"Let me guess, stun arrows?"

"Precisely. Sometimes you may not want to kill someone that's annoying you, or for that matter, not annoying you. Either way, one hit with this and they'll be completely but temporarily" she emphasized knowing Aloy would appreciate it more, "paralyzed".

"How did you even make this?"

"It involved a lot of alcohol."

Aloy cocked her head.

"I don't remember" Petra said.

"Well, they would be useful."

"I was hoping you'd say that. I already made about fifty of them."

"What would you have done if I said no?" she asked quizzically.

"Probably throw em' at whoever annoyed me the most."

"I'll take them."

The forgewoman beamed before returning to gather the rest of them.

"And Petra" she called before she ran off, "Thank you."

END.

-Acknowledgements-

Thanks to Gurella for making such a great game. All characters belong to them. This is only a fan made story to continue Aloy's journey.

Printed in Great Britain
by Amazon